A POTPOURRI OF STORIES AND TALES

Growing up on Country Roads—the title of my unfinished memoir—and traveling countless throughfares across the world, bequeathed a wealth of experiences and memories that fill me up. Oh, but then, I must add the daughter, Chris who died too young, and son, Mitch who bestowed on me paramount joys and tender moments. I glow with the blessings of grandchildren and great grandchildren as we hike a mountain, bake a loaf of bread, celebrate a milestone, or aim for tomorrow. Add then, the thousands of eager or uncertain faces that touched my soul during the over sixty years I've spent in classrooms, plus singing joyous songs with choirs for almost forever. Can't forget friendships galore during years of playing bridge, domino games, sharing meals together—rooms filled with laughter and ofttimes, tears. And above all, my cup runneth over with the blessings of faith in My God, My Savior Jesus, and the Holy Spirit. Is it no wonder that I desire to tell a story, to spin a tale?

A POTPOURRI OF STORIES AND TALES

(A LITTLE SPICE, ZEST, SWEET, PUNGENT, TART, OR TANG)

CAROL ALFORD

Primix Publishing
11620 Wilshire Blvd
Suite 900, West Wilshire Center, Los Angeles, CA, 90025
www.primixpublishing.com
Phone: 1-800-538-5788

© 2023 Carol Alford. All rights reserved.

No part of this book may be reproduced, stored in a retrieval system, or transmitted by any means without the written permission of the author.

Published by Primix Publishing   11/01/2023

ISBN: 979-8-89194-018-5(sc)
ISBN: 979-8-89194-019-2(e)

Library of Congress Control Number: 2023919085

Any people depicted in stock imagery provided by iStock are models, and such images are being used for illustrative purposes only.

Certain stock imagery © iStock.

Because of the dynamic nature of the Internet, any web addresses or links contained in this book may have changed since publication and may no longer be valid. The views expressed in this work are solely those of the author and do not necessarily reflect the views of the publisher, and the publisher hereby disclaims any responsibility for them.

DEDICATION

I dedicate A Potpourri of Stories and Tales (a little spice, zest, sweet, pungent, tart, or tang) to my son Mitchell Edward Crockett who shares his joy for others with his charismatic personality, but mostly from his loving heart. Indeed, he understands spice, zest, sweet, pungent, tart or tang in life as well.

CONTENTS

MAYHEM AT MOUNTAIN RIDGES 1
THE RETRIEVAL OF SANITY 24
THE HUDDLING PLACE 26
AREA CODE 970 30
FULL CIRCLE 56
THE FACE OF A SUNBEAM 61
THE DAMSEL'S DESIRE 64

MAYHEM AT MOUNTAIN RIDGES

By Carol Alford

Clang! Clunk! Clang! Good gravy. She's back.
       Maggie Grant lifted her head from the pillow and twisted her body to sit on the side of her bed in her 25-foot Jayco motorhome. Summer was waning and she'd seen the bear that she dubbed the Black Phantom come through the campground many times. The Phantom came before sunrise and pawed at the dumpsters near her RV, trying to bang the bear locks open.
       MG, as she liked to be called, watched through the bedroom window at the rear of her rig. As before, the shadowy bulk made one attempt after another before she gave up and wobbled between the pine trees and out of sight. As a host at Mountain Ridges Campground, MG, all five foot two of her, was savvy in dealing with bears, and Phantom's roaming caused her no alarm. She worried about the visitors though. Some ran screaming from wildlife. Others got too close for photos or tried to entice chipmunks, bears or moose with Cheetos, lettuce, or other foods.
       MG stepped from her motorhome and drank in the pine-infused air and heard the rush of the river below. *How I love it.* Since the campground meandered for a mile along the Poudre River in northern Colorado, her host job kept her busy servicing many camp sites. The

youthful fifty-two-year-old had even been known to back a fifth-wheel RV into the campsite when the truck driver pulling the RV scored an F in backing.

She gathered her tools to begin the morning chores at space #49. Leaning over the fire pit ring, MG's hands flew as she shoveled chunks of burned logs. When she reached the gritty ashes, a swirl of black soot whirled up into her eyes. *Damn.* Would she ever be able to do this job without "wearing" half of the ashes she worked to clear away? MG blinked the tears from her stinging eyeballs and grabbed the metal pronged rake. In minutes she had twigs, leaves, wayward pine needles and bits of partially burned newspaper in a neat pile.

Rueben, her co-worker, forever told her to slow down. She hated people telling her what to do. Didn't he know that work was not work to her? It was invigorating. She had enjoyed her last fourteen years with the USDA as a veterinarian traveling from one state to another coordinating information about scrapie, a disease associated with sheep and goats. Before that, she'd worked as a vet in a small animal practice and even found that sick and dying doggies didn't get her down.

MG left the USDA when her husband Blake dumped her for his law associate. She forged a new life, a fresh beginning. Being a full-timer living in her RV meant new adventures and travel experiences ahead. This was her first gig as a campground host, and she planned to do a stint in Texas once winter came. In addition to being a camp host, MG had begun writing fiction on the side—another new beginning, a desire that had been on the back burner for a few years.

Vroom, blubb, blubb, blubbb. What the heck? Who's invading my campground? Shiny, red, and black with extra saddle bags, a Kawasaki Vulcan 1600 motorcycle pulling a cargo trailer stopped in front of the campsite. Because Blake, her ex-husband, had been into motorcycles she judged this one to be at least ten years old. A clean-shaven young man, maybe mid-twenties, climbed from the cycle and helped a shapely blond gal dismount from the back.

He stepped toward MG and nodded. "Ma'am, are you the head honcho here? We're looking to find a tent camp spot for a while."

"Head honcho, huh?" MG laughed. "I'm on duty today. Most sites are booked, but we have a few open tent spaces to check out. By the way, young man, where's your helmet?"

He offered his hand to shake MG's. "Don't use one Ma'am. I'm Jesse."

MG removed her sooty glove and took Jesse's hand. What a firm and confident grip, she thought, then said, "Living dangerously, huh?"

Jesse shrugged and turned toward the young woman with a smile. "This is Annika. She's from Sweden and I'm showing her our country. We hope to hang out in the Colorado Rockies for a while."

"We have a lot of country here to see. Nice to meet you two. My name is Maggie Grant, but you can call me MG."

Jesse nodded, "MG, huh? Well, OK. Can you show us what you have, MG?"

"It's quite a walk, but you can tell me a bit about yourselves and get the feel for the area on the way, if that's OK."

"I feel quite at home," said Annika, stretching her arms toward the trees lining the road. "Many of Sweden's forests have pine and spruce trees, similar to these."

"Interesting. Well, let's get going."

The threesome ambled along the paved winding road toward the far west loop to explore the tenting area. People often opened up to MG and today was no different. She learned that Jesse grew up in California and after he completed a business degree at age 22, he hired on with a small winery to learn the business. During his three-year stint, he experienced the whole gamut, from managing the vineyard to harvesting and processing the grapes, helping oversee the fermentation procedure and bottling. Once, he had saved a chunk of change—his words—he flew to Hawaii and got a job. Annika's father, a Swedish diplomat and widower, sent Annika to Hawaii to get away from a scary and obsessive dating relationship.

"Annika had a room a block from the Buns of Maui shop where I worked. She came in every morning for coffee and a bun." Jesse eyed the blue-eyed beauty. "And it didn't take long to become friends."

"He was a great help," said Annika, "negotiating the intricacies of getting a job. In no time I had a part time waitress job. They assured me I'd get more hours soon. My father said he'd send money for living expenses, but I wanted to make it on my own."

"That's tough to do, especially in Maui," said MG. "The cost of living is over the moon."

"We did well though," said Jesse. "Annika moved to my place. We hoped to stay a year or two, living on a shoestring, shopping the local markets, cooking our own food."

Annika grinned and nodded. "Yeah, Jesse's a fantastic cook. I learned a lot. But I'm the workout nut, so we hiked all over the island."

"Then why are you here? Did you get itchy to move on?"

The couple stared at each other. Annika sighed. "Shall we tell her?"

Jesse nodded. "It wasn't exactly our choice." He bit his lip and grimaced. "Annika noticed some jerk following her."

"It wasn't anyone I knew, some local—a native of the island. I asked what he wanted, why he was following me. He laughed and said it was none of my business. Then he walked away."

"I work early making and baking cinnabuns, so Annika always stopped in before she headed to her restaurant job. A couple of days after the confrontation, I was busy in the back. Annika poured her coffee and pulled up a chair."

Annika's voice quivered. "Then the jerk came in, got himself a coffee and sat at my table. He grilled me about Jesse's and my relationship. Asked how long we would stay in Hawaii, when I planned to return to Sweden. I freaked and refused to talk to him. All the while he smiled his wicked smile."

"When I came out from the back and saw Annika's face, I realized this was the stalker. He was a big guy, lots of muscle. But I had to do something. I grabbed my phone and snapped a picture of him, then stomped over and told him to leave. He left, but not before he stood, shoved the table across the room and warned me that he could snap my neck in one move."

MG shook her head. "Scary! Did you go to the police?"

"We did. I had his picture on my phone, but they weren't too optimistic about finding the guy and we had no idea why he targeted Annika. And so openly."

"Is that why you left Maui?"

"Not then," said Annika, "we weren't going to let some nobody control our lives. We worked out a way to signal the cops if he showed up again. But that didn't happen, and we took a deep breath of relief. Decided he was some weirdo, and he was out of our lives."

"Some mystery, huh?" MG thought of the novel she was writing. Her villain was a weirdo. *Would I be scared off by a weirdo? No way. I'd hunt him down.* "I guess you decided to take no chances and left Maui."

"Not yet," said Annika. "When I found a dead cockatiel, poor thing, on my pillow, I decided the weirdo wasn't out of our lives." Annika's chest heaved and she spoke in feverish staccato. "Then we found *whore and bitch* scrawled on the door in red paint. I was hopping mad and felt violated."

Jesse cut in. "The worst was yet to come. Viktor, the ex-boyfriend, arrived on the island. We think he hired the weirdo to find Annika. The Ex attacked Annika as she left work. He dragged her to a car in the parking lot."

"Oh no! What happened?"

Jesse wrapped his arm around Annika's shoulder and pulled her close to his side. He smiled. "Can you believe this Swedish lass escaped?"

"Well, I took a few self-defense classes," said Annika. "The groin maneuver and eye gouging did the trick before I ran."

As the threesome continued their trek toward the tent spots, MG learned that Annika's father hired a Hawaiian private detective and a guard immediately. Even so, the ex-boyfriend slipped away, and the private detective discovered he returned to Sweden. There was nothing to be done about the Hawaiian encounter because of foreign jurisdiction—Sweden couldn't do anything about an attack in Hawaii. MG imagined the couple fleeing the island. Life wasn't fair. Had the couple covered their tracks as well as they thought? Was Viktor really out of their lives? Regardless, MG assured them as long as they were settled in *her* campground, they would be safe. She hoped she could live up to that declaration.

MG awoke early Tuesday to the Phantom's wrestling with the garbage cans. This was becoming a daily routine for the black bear. Other than checking new reservations with her satellite system, which she reported to Rueben so he could date and tag camping spots, today was MG's day off. By nine in the morning, she had put in her two hours of writing and had only three pages to show for it. She might as well get the updated registration information to Rueben.

With the printed documents in hand, she climbed into her golf cart and found Rueben and his wife outside the restroom and shower building. Very few mountain campgrounds had such a building, which partially accounted for the campground's popularity. She liked Gladys well enough, but knew the woman slacked when it came to cleaning the building and servicing the shower coin machines. It irked MG when campers complained that there was no toilet paper or no change for the machines.

MG climbed from the golf cart and waved the reservation schedules. "Things aren't slowing down. Looks like we'll be full for the next month. Only a few available spaces for drive-ins mid-week. All the spaces, except a few tent sites, are reserved for every weekend."

"What about those tenters that came in yesterday?" asked Rueben. "I noticed they had a nice campfire going last night when I checked their loop."

"I'm heading that way now to chat with them. Nice couple. They plan to hike some of the nearby trails. I want to give them a heads up. I noticed the signage to Jonas Rock is missing. That trail can be a little tricky."

Rueben scanned the schedules. "Thanks. By the way, the couple in that pull through at site 29 has a request. Their dog, a fluffy one—don't know my breeds— has lumps on its neck and acts sick. I told them you're a vet and could look at it for them."

"Rueben, you know I haven't had a small animal practice for fifteen years."

"I'd guess being a vet is like riding a bicycle, you never forget. Besides, you're pretty smart about most things."

Buttering me up again, she thought. And yes, she *could* check out the pooch and give her opinion, but they'd have to wait.

"Well, I'll see what I can do later, but now I want to visit the new tenters."

"OK, I get it." When Ruben heard an engine rumble, he looked up and ran his hand over his gray crew cut. "Wonder what the Forest Service guys want today. This isn't the day for their rounds."

MG watched the green truck pull up in front of them. "Yeah, I wonder too." Two men climbed from the truck. She knew Officer Troy Hawes, but the other man wasn't familiar. As the men stepped closer, she noticed that the new guy was a county sheriff deputy. "Hey, Troy, what goes?"

"Hi, MG. Hi, Gladys and Rueben. This is Deputy Tomas." Troy sighed. "Some bad news. Be on the lookout for an escaped prisoner. He was being extradited to Utah, charged with rape and assault, maybe even murder."

Deputy Tomas cut in. "A cunning bastard. While being transported, the prisoner had to use the head. He attacked the guard and chained him to a bathroom stall. We're certain he's heading into the mountains away from the highway. He's considered dangerous. I'm riding with Officer Hawes, since all our deputies are scattered throughout the area. We're warning everyone we can. Up here, unless the rigs are equipped with satellite, your people wouldn't get the news."

"Shoot," said Rueben. "We don't want some crazy dude breaking into a trailer or fifth wheel or attacking a patron at night. What's the guy look like?"

Deputy Tomas pulled a photo from an envelope. Piercing dark eyes stared out beneath an unruly shock of dark hair. A full beard covered his face but did not hide his sneer. "You can see his mugshot," said the deputy, "on Denver TV stations, but ..." He waved his arm toward the mountainside. "No coverage here. This is all I have."

"By golly," said MG, "he's a mean looker. He could change his appearance easily with all that hair. Have you sent dogs out yet?"

"The attacker is hours ahead of us. But the dogs arrived at the escape scene 20 minutes ago. These things take time. Let's get the word out here ASAP."

"What do you think MG?" said Rueben. "Would it help to make some copies of the mug shot to pass around? You have your scanner and printer."

"Let's give it a try. It won't take me long. We can make our rounds of the campground, give them the news, and have something to hand to them. Can you guys help us get the word out?"

Troy gave MG a wary look. "We'd sure like to, but we have a lot of stops to make up the canyon. Lots of riverside cabins and more campgrounds."

"I'll hurry then." MG returned in minutes and handed Troy the original photo. "You have the number for my satellite cell. Keep us informed."

Inside her rig, MG listened to the swishing sound as the copy machine thrust each page into the tray. She found herself counting each swish and shook her head. *What a senseless habit, always counting… steps or how long I have to sit at a red light. I guess that's me.*

Still counting, she walked to the back of her rig and lifted the hinged platform holding the mattress. She appreciated the extra hidden storage space. It was a stretch to grasp the bundle tucked in the corner. *Come here, baby.* She had never owned a pistol, but when she decided to RV full-time and become a campground host, she bought a Colt King Cobra and obtained the proper permits to carry. Spending several days at the shooting range, she found that she had a steady hand, firm grip and hit the target accurately 8 out of 10 times. Despite her ability, she didn't like the idea of people on the street carrying. Thus, this was the first time she pulled out the cobra. *I guess it's time for me to carry.* By the time the copy machine quieted, and she stopped counting, she had the gun in its shoulder holster under her armpit with a loose-fitting flannel shirt hiding the weapon. *Am I being overly cautious, paranoid, or shrewd?* Tempted to remove the holster, she unbuttoned the top buttons of her shirt. Shaking her head, she rebuttoned them and hurried on.

MG grabbed the stack of 66 copied mug shots, enough facsimiles for each RV and tent space, plus a few extras. She bounded down the steps of her Jayco and waved them toward Ruben, who waited at her picnic table. Once she divvied up the stack and they decided Ruben would take the first 27 spaces, MG jumped on her golf cart and drove to double camping site at #28. A luxury Dutch Star motor coach dwarfed the pop-up trailer to its right.

MG had visited with the Kingstons who drove from Oregon to spend time with their son, daughter-in-law and three grandchildren in Colorado. Though she had none of her own, MG got on well with children, particularly the young ones. The day after they arrived, MG had helped the 6-year-old twin boys and their 4-year-old sister gather pinecones for their campfire. The little sister was a firecracker who dashed lickety-split and collected twice as many as her brothers. It reminded MG of herself at that age. How she hated to break the news to this precious family.

MG didn't see anyone at the site but yelled through the screen door of the Dutch Star, "Hello, Mr. Kingston, it's Maggie Grant. Can I speak with you?"

After a bit of rustling inside, Mrs. Kingston opened the screen door and stepped outside. "Why hello Maggie. The children wanted to go on a 'real mountain hike' they said. They even took a lunch in their backpacks. So, I'm the only one here. Kind of enjoying the quiet... actually. Do you want to come in?"

"Thank you, but no. I'm making the rounds to alert everyone about an escaped convict who could be hiding out in the mountains." MG handed her the picture she had copied and explained more about the fugitive and then added, "We don't want to frighten anyone, but it pays to stay close and be on the lookout."

"Do you think I should try to find the family and warn them?"

A rush of air whistled between MG's gritted teeth. "I'd stay put. Your loved ones are in a group, and with the young'uns they should return before too long. I wouldn't head off hiking alone, particularly if you're unfamiliar with the terrain. We'll give you updates when we have them."

Oh dear, I wasn't thinking. Should've given Ruben the next one. The one with the doggie. "Good morning," said MG as she stepped onto the campsite. A middle-aged woman sat in a foldup recliner cuddling a ball of fur.

She yelled out, "Hank, the campground host, the vet is here to check out Tinka."

MG watched Hank come from behind the motor home carrying a doggie bowl of water. "Thank God. We need to know what to do with our pooch. Usually, she's hopping on her back feet doing tricks. Not anymore. Then Suzie noticed those lumps on her neck."

MG grimaced. "Well, OK, let me take a look. Can you put Tinka on the picnic table? She's sure a cutie. A Shih Tzu, right?"

Hank nodded. "Now that we're empty-nesters, she's our delight."

Sad, tired eyes peeked back at MG through a white and black fringe. "You're not feeling good, are you?" The little dog whimpered as she tenderly worked her fingers through the silky hair. "It's hard to tell what's going on. She definitely has swollen lymph nodes here on her neck. It could mean an infection from something like diseased teeth, a more serious fungal or bacterial infection, auto-immune problem or even cancer."

Suzie leaned in to kiss the Shih Tzu. With a sniff, she spoke, "What can you do for her?"

"Nothing, really. You need to take her to a vet for some tests. They'll do some bloodwork and a tick titer test to rule out some conditions. Then probably a needle aspiration. I wouldn't wait. Once you leave the mountains you can google a vet in Fort Collins."

Hank reached out to shake MG's hand. "Thank you so much. We'll leave right away."

"Glad to help. But there's something else I need to tell you before you go."

She handed the picture to the couple, explained the situation, and made her way to the next campsites. Reactions varied from *we're not sticking around to meet up with a dangerous criminal to* a shrug and *thanks for the info, but we don't think the guy'll care about scouring our campground.*

When she reached the tenting area, the sun hovered high overhead. Several campers cooked over an open fire while others split wood or lazed in hammocks. She called the group together and completed her spiel. Like some of the others, they didn't have much reaction, rather sloughed it off. Disappointed by the absence of Jesse and Annika, MG gestured to their camp, "Anyone know about this couple?"

"Yeah," one camper said, "they left early morning. Wanted to explore Jonas Rock." The man looked up the mountainside. "I guess it's up that way."

MG breathed heavily and chewed on her lip. "Thanks. Think I'll check the trail. I know it was damaged and some of the signs were lost last year in a flash flood. Have a good day." She waved at the group and trudged up the trail.

Roots, downed trees, and rocks littered the pathway. A few broken pieces of signage jutted from crusted mounds of dirt. The trails and directional signs had been damaged in the raging downpour last year and made the trail difficult to identify. *It would be easy to veer off and lose your way. I hope Annika and Jesse aren't lost.* A ranger had led her to the rock after she arrived in April, so she had a pretty good idea about which offshoot to take. The ranger assured her the trail would be repaired during the summer, but it hadn't happened.

Jonas Rock stood as a pinnacle on a high outcropping and provided amazing views of white capped peaks in the distance, a meadow to the east and a trickling stream below that would eventually find its way to the Poudre River. As she reached the halfway point, MG remembered sitting in the solitude atop the mammoth rock as sweet breezes whispered by. Embraced by the vastness before her, she cherished the peace, calm and steadiness within. Later she attempted to identify the sensations stirring in her being and could not find the words.

The trail grew more rigorous, and she stopped to draw in deep breaths in the high altitude. Off to the left she heard voices and the crunching of branches. As the sounds faded in and out, she heard at least one female voice. *Could it be Annika and Jesse?* She tucked her arm against her weapon and then admonished herself. *There's no danger.*

"Hello," she yelled out. "Annika? Jesse? Are you there? It's MG. Come toward my voice. Over here."

The excited chatter drew closer until two sweaty figures crashed through the heavy brush. "MG," Annika called out, "so glad you yelled at us. We thought we'd never find our way back."

Jesse gave MG a sideways grin. "We never made it to Jonas Rock. Got off trail, I guess. Well, I knew if we kept moving downhill, we'd get somewhere, sometime."

"Guess what?" started Annika. "We found a cabin. It was far off. It looked deserted, but then we spotted some guy leaving the with a rifle. Is this hunting season?"

MG shook her head. "Not until fall. What did the guy look like? We've had a situation here and we need to be cautious."

"It was hard to tell," Jesse said. "We weren't very close. Looked more like a hermit. He moved pretty fast though, not like an old guy. Dark clothes. I think a beard."

MG pulled the folded picture from her pocket and explained about the escaped fugitive. Wide eyes stared back at her. "Can't tell if it's him," said Jesse, "but I'd say the beard might be a clue. Gees, what if it's the guy and he's found a gun and clothes at the cabin?" asked Jesse.

"Hard telling, but we need to get back to the campground, check on updates and report what you saw," said MG.

At the campground, MG learned that the dogs had lost the fugitive's scent due to high winds about nine miles downstream from the campground. The sheriff had no evidence that he was heading toward the campground but encouraged caution. The deputies would check out the cabin the young couple had seen.

Following a restless sleep, MG rose early the next morning hoping to get a few pages of her novel completed. It was her day off, but she had things she wanted to do in and outside of her rig. As dawn arrived, she listened for Phantom Lady, but all remained quiet. Shuffling around the small kitchen, still wearing the loungers that served as her sleep wear, she set the coffee pot to on and waited for the brew to trickle into her giant mug. She needed something to rev her system that had taken a slowdown with lack of sleep.

Some unusual sounds startled her. *What the? Was that a shot? An animal in trouble?* She yanked on her sneakers, grabbed the neoprene shoulder holster with the Colt King Cobra, and wrapped the band around her upper body. Deftly pressing the Velcro pieces together, MG flew out the door and scrambled toward the rocky hill behind her rig. Hitting the ground one foot at a time with violent determination, she slipped and fell to her knees more than once. She heard two more shots up the hill and to the right. *That has to be a rifle.* She clambered in that direction. Then caution kicked in. *Sheesh, what am I doing?* MG paused, gripped her Colt and pulled it from the holster. Moving gingerly in a half-crouched position she inched toward an outcropping of boulders and rocks. Eyes shifting from side to side she felt like a cougar stalking a downed animal. A metallic taste filled her mouth as she worked her tongue over her teeth. *Come on, don't get all scaredy-cat now. It's either go over the boulders or around them.* Then she thought of Blake, her ex-husband, and smiled. *If he could only see me now.*

Fingers squeezing the pistol grip, MG pulled the colt close to her chest as she avoided the massive boulders and wound her way through tangled shrubbery. She grabbed branches to pull them aside with her free hand. *Damn thorns.* Blood seeped from torn skin and formed red bracelet stripes before she dabbed what she could with the hem of her knit lounger shirt. *Why didn't I put on jeans and boots?*

Finally, out of the brambles MG emerged into a clearing surrounded by low growing junipers and tall pines. She spun toward the sound, a low growl, barely audible, and raised her pistol, pulling the hammer back. Her mouth hung open at the sight not 20 yards from her. A crumped black furry mass slumped against the rock laden terrain. At one end of the mass, a head bobbed ever so slightly.

"Oh, Phantom Lady. Who did this to you?" Reaching the beautiful specimen, MG squatted beside her. Blood oozed from her neck and shoulder. Much had already puddled around the animal. Again, a low growl gurgled from the bear's throat. MG's eyes blinked against her flowing tears, yet her gaze continued to focus on Phantom Lady's eyes, eyes of sadness, pain, and pleading.

"No, fine lady, I can't do it." MG placed her pistol in its holster and sat beside her black bear friend, rocking in her own grief. Minute after minute passed as the creature fought for one breath and another. A rustling breeze shook the trees and Phantom Lady shuddered her last breath.

The saddened woman pulled herself to an erect stance, hands on hips. Anger simmered beneath her own breath. She threw her hands over her head and bellowed out to the dawn-filled sky, "I'll get you, you murderer. Some way I will."

"MG, is that you? I'm heading your way."

MG heard footsteps tramp closer to her from the direction of the voice. Propelling herself between two stately pines, Annika stopped and glared with ferocity at the scene before her.

"Oh no. Oh no," cried Annika, shaking her head with vehemence. "Did you …?"

"No. Never. But I *will* get the guy who did this. First, I need to change my loungers and put on my hiking boots."

Annika stepped toward the beautiful beast and knelt to stroke her glistening hair. "She was a beauty." And then, shooting a look toward MG, Annika said, "I'm coming with you."

As the pair trudged down the mountain toward the campground, MG learned that Jesse had taken the motorcycle down the canyon to pick up some groceries, while Annika, all decked out in hiking clothes and boots, intended to talk to MG to inquire about a new hiking trail. Annika had heard the shots and scurried up the mountain in that direction and had found MG and the slain Phantom Lady.

"Do you think the escapee killed your bear?"

MG smiled at the reference of 'your bear.' Yes, the bear was her friend, and she would miss her. "I don't know. Maybe. But why would he shoot her?"

"Why do evil men do anything? Maybe she was in his way. What's your plan MG? What are you thinking?"

"I called about the cabin and that guy you saw. My ranger friend Troy said someone from the sheriff's department would come to check it out. When, I don't know. You'd think they'd want to follow up on every lead immediately. I guess I'll have to do their work for them."

"Not without me. I'm coming with you."

MG shook her head. "I can't let you take such a risk. It's my job to keep all of you safe."

"Well, Maggie Grant—yes, I remember your full name—and when my mom used my full name, she meant business. I mean business. I'm tougher than you think and who knows what you'll find? Two are better than one in my book."

MG heaved a heavy sigh. "We'll see."

As the pair arrived at MG's Host Campsite, she turned toward Annika, "You can wait out here. I won't be long, just need a quick change of clothes."

Inside, MG pulled off her loungers and grabbed her jeans and a long-sleeved shirt. As she pushed her second foot into the leg of her jeans, she heard a commotion outside and then a heavy rap on her door.

"MG, you're needed out here," yelled Annika.

"Now what?" MG uttered under her breath, as she finished dressing.

Jumping from her motor home, she nearly rammed into Hank and Suzie, the owners of the sick doggie, Tinka. "Oh, dear, what's going on?"

A rush of words spilled from Suzie. "Someone broke into our rig. Our door lock is damaged, and food is gone, Hank's coat and what else Hank?"

"Our backpacks, both of them."

Suzie cut in again. "We took Tinka to the vet yesterday and decided to rent a motel, rather than come back in the dark. Just came in this morning, ten minutes ago."

"So sorry about that. I'm just leaving to check on some things myself. I'll use my satellite system to report the break in before I go. Need a locksmith?"

"I have a batch of tools and parts. I've worked on all kinds of mishaps with our rig. I can work on the lock. Don't worry about the door," said Hank.

MG jabbed one number and then another on her satellite phone and waited. Oh damn. She hated the dial one if… dial two if… routine. She pressed number three and heard Troy's answering mechanism pick up.

"Troy, MG. We have a situation at the campground. I need you to report a motorhome break-in to the sheriff. The thief broke the lock, stole clothes, food, and backpacks. It's got to be the escapee. And what's going on with the sheriff? I thought someone would be here to check out the cabin I reported about. Well, I guess I'll have to take care of my people myself. Can't depend on law enforcement."

MG went back into her rig, holstered her pistol in the shoulder apparatus, grabbed a canvas bag, tossed some things into the bag, and looped the straps over her head to secure the bag. She jumped from her rig and jerked her head toward Annika. "Let's go."

Annika grinned. "You bet. What's in the bag?"

"My bag of tricks. I think I know where the cabin is and maybe you can remember some key landmarks."

"So, you're thinking that the escaped prisoner broke into Suzie and Hank's rig, stole food and other stuff."

"That's what I'm thinking. Probably filled the backpacks with the food and headed toward the cabin."

"Hmm. That might be the motive. Your bear smelled the food … Yeah, we have to get that guy."

MG and Annika tromped the trail that snaked up the mountainside in hairpin turns, sometimes vanishing in washed out ruts and rocks, and then again returning to a distinct path. MG's mind whirled. *Why didn't I tell Rueben where I was going? Should I have told Hank to stay out of the rig until the Sheriff Deputy could check for prints? But would someone from the sheriff's department even come? Maybe in three days. Why did I allow Annika to come with me? What if the prisoner is squatting at the cabin? Then what?*

Pushing the spinning thoughts aside, MG concentrated on the path. "I haven't noticed any particular footprints, Annika. Have you?"

"No."

MG continued, "Of course, we could have this thing all wrong. Someone else, not the escapee, broke into the rig. And then, there are hundreds of ways to make it up the mountainside if the thief headed up. Does anything look familiar to you? See anything that you saw on your hike?"

Annika stopped, hands on hips, and made a 360, surveying the area. "Wait. There." Annika pointed to the right. "I remember that boulder. About the size of a bus. The one stacked with a big flat rock and a round one on top. Jesse said it looked like a bus carrying a giant cup and saucer."

"OK… Hmm. Think we're near the cabin?"

Annika licked her lips and squinted. She grinned with a nod. "Follow me."

Annika led MG around the group of boulders and into a clearing cloaked in knee high grasses. At the far side of the clearing, the pair spotted the corner of a weather-worn log structure hidden in a stand of aspen.

"That's it. The place we saw the man. Can't see the door from here, but it's around the corner."

MG pulled Annika back into the shadows of the forest. "Well, we know someone has been there, but who? And is he there now? For sure we need to stay under cover until we know more. We could sit here all day and not learn a thing."

"Want me to circle around to the back of the cabin for a look?" asked Annika.

"There are all kinds of logging roads winding in these hills. I'd like to check out the area. You stay here while I loop to the left to see what I can find." MG looked at her watch. "It's 9:40. I'll be back in 45 minutes or so. You keep watch."

MG moved like a panther, keeping in the forest shadows as she continued her loop around the clearing. A blend of pines, spruces and firs surrounded her and soon she could no longer see the aspen grove where the cabin stood. Surely, she would find a logging road that would lead to the cabin. Whoever owned it had to have some access. She climbed over fallen trees of Lodgepole Pine and skirted around dead ones, not yet toppled by wind, forging her own path hoping to circle around the cabin area. Ahead she spotted three—almost perfectly shaped— Blue Spruce. Always her favorite conifer, and Colorado's state tree, she had watched such trees grow from five-footers to stately adults in her family's yard during her childhood. *Could this be some omen?*

She trudged forward and, in a few minutes stumbled into a rough, heavily rutted logging road cutting through the forest. Turning right she followed the road for a couple of hundred yards. Yup, she remembered exploring the logging area when she first arrived but hadn't gotten this far. Troy said the locals named it Gerneys road, for an early logger. MG noticed orange flags attached to trees along the way with numbers sprayed on the trees. She had no idea what the numbers meant.

She came upon a clear-cut area. Loggers had removed an old stand of Ponderosa Pine. MG made her way across it hoping to arrive somewhere behind the cabin. Rotting stumps dotted the site, along with young saplings, some reaching as high as her chest. Nearing the edge of the clear-cut section, she stopped. Some noises in the forest alerted her. *An animal? A person?*

She ducked down and drilled her eyes in the direction of the rustling sounds. A shadowy form moved from the shaded forest into full sunlight. MG parted the branches of a sapling to get a better view. *He has to be the bearded criminal.* The man paused to reposition his load. *Aha. The backpacks and the rifle that killed Phantom Lady. Gotcha.*

MG's breathing came in quick spurts while her heart pounded. *OK, calm down. You need to think this through. Can't let him get away.*

Minutes later, MG watched the man secure the backpacks in place and prop the rifle over his shoulder. He scoured the scene from side to side. Then he started off. MG read his plan to circumvent the clear-cut section and stay close to the forested area—for protection she imagined. He could reach the logging road, which would be faster traveling, in twenty minutes or so. Should she try to get ahead of him and intercept him? Surprise him? Could she do this alone?

Inching up a bit, MG watched the man's back as he moved on. She gazed around her. *What was that?* Not far from the spot where the criminal had exited the forest, MG spotted a bit of color. Turquoise blue. Straining her eyes in that direction a figure in turquoise blue darted from one tree to another. Annika. *What are you doing? Go back.* She couldn't yell out. What should she do? Then the figure disappeared.

No time to lose, MG half crawled, and crept in a squat position until she reached the edge of the new growth and snuck into the forest. She hoped the criminal would use the logging road. He had to. She would get ahead of him. She went into hurry-up mode. The terrain dipped and swooped, then leveled out. She hit a spot littered with branches, loose stones, and pine needles, lost her footing, and slid on her back side down the hill. Thrusting her boot against a tree, she ended her skid. Sitting for a moment, she listened for any sounds. Nothing.

Refusing to give in to her tailbone discomfort, she pushed onward. In desperation she murmured under her breath. "Hey, Lord, you're going to have to help me with this. I might be in over my head."

A few minutes later she stopped in her tracks. *My trees.* The Blue Spruce loomed before her. She knew where she was. Knew she needed to rush ahead to make certain she could intercept the bad man. At a jog, she dodged around one tree and another, keeping the logging road in sight. The logging road narrowed, and gigantic boulders loomed on each side. This was the spot. If she caught him between the boulders, it would be difficult to escape. What would she do? Jump out in front of him and aim her pistol at him. An image of a shootout at the OK Corral flashed through her head. She almost laughed at herself. Ambush him from above?

MG crossed the road and climbed on the boulders there, hoping to find the perfect spot for the ambush. She heard a rustle in the woods in front of her. *Good gravy.* A splash of turquoise caught her eye.

In a hushed voice MG called out, "Annika." She scrambled off the mammoth rocks and ran toward the younger woman.

Annika's words came in a rush. "We made it. We're here together. We don't have much time. I followed for a while and then moved through the trees to get ahead of him. He's heading this way."

In a few minutes, the pair took their places, waiting. Gripping her weapon, MG peered through the stack of juniper branches the pair had quickly piled to hide her from view. Annika remained out of sight. Minutes ticked off. *What if he takes a different route?*

Then she saw him before she heard him. His pace was quick. Timing needed to be perfect. The evil man passed in front of her, carrying the rifle to his side in his left hand. MG held her breath. Then the diversion.

Annika limped, dragging her right foot onto the road, and halted ten feet in front of the man. A disheveled mess, dirt covered, she cried out in a pathetic voice, "Help, I'm injured. Water. Need water." She staggered a few more feet forward.

"What the?... Can't help you missy. Get out of my way," the man growled.

MG jumped behind the man and raised a heavy limb ready to smash it into the back of his head. At the last nanosecond he turned, and the weapon cracked against his forehead with a hefty force. His shriek echoed throughout the forest. He lost his balance and the rifle skittered to the ground. Annika went into action. She reached the stunned figure in a flash, gripped his head with both hands and jabbed dirty thumbs into his eyes, then with immense power thrust her knee into his groin. The man stumbled forward, roaring like a lion.

Again, MG swung the limb. It caught the man on his left cheek and ear. He went down. He tossed off the backpacks and crawled forward.

"You bitches. I'll kill you both."

Annika grabbed the rifle and aimed it at the struggling man. "Don't move or I'll shoot."

MG stepped away, just as she saw the man grip a flash of silver. Probably a hunting knife, she thought.

Annika yelled again, "She might not shoot you, but I will. Drop it."

Bloody and wounded the man was not giving up. He lunged toward Annika. She backed away and aimed. Crack. The bullet whizzed past him and shattered against the boulder, spraying pieces of rock in every direction.

"This one's for my bear." Looming from behind, MG wielded the limb once more. It cut into his bicep and sent the knife flying. For good measure, MG wacked him across the back. Flailing on the ground the man let out a thunder of profanity.

MG pulled her pistol from its shoulder holster and handed it to Annika. "Shoot him in the knee if he moves." She retrieved her bag of tricks from its hiding place. Before the suffering man could resist, MG kicked the man to his stomach and secured his wrists together with heavy-duty zip-lock ties. She sat on the man's legs and zip-tied his ankles together and pushed his face into the dirt. "That should hold you till the authorities get here. Oh, yeah, one more thing."

MG continued, "Need a little help here, Annika." The pair dragged the immobilized man to the side of the road, sat him against the lone tree growing beside the group of boulders, and used the rope from MG's bag to tie him to the tree.

"I think it's time to report in." MG lifted her satellite phone from her bag.

"You thought of everything in your bag of tricks, didn't you?"

This time Troy answered. After hearing of the events and that they had the criminal restrained, and after giving MG a good scolding, Troy said he knew how to get to Guerneys road, and they would be there in an hour or so.

"Hungry?" MG looked at her watch. "It's about noon."

"I am. And thirsty too."

Rummaging through the backpacks MG found numerous canned goods, deli meats, a box of crackers, a squashed loaf of bread, apples, oranges, and bottles of water. "Let's find a spot away from this awful creature. I don't like looking at him and listening to his cussing, growling, and grumbling."

The pair settled in a spot down the road from the ambush scene and enjoyed a needed feast.

"I see you don't follow directions very well. I told you to wait until I got back." MG eyed Annika with a smirky grin.

"And what if I had?" Annika returned her own smirky grin. "I decided to sneak to the cabin. When I got there, I heard all kinds of commotion inside. I didn't dare look in the window, as smoky as it was, so I just stayed close. When he took off, I followed. What else could I do?"

"What a coincidence that we ended up in the same place," said MG.

"Well, that wasn't such a coincidence."

"What do you mean by that?"

"I saw you in that area where the new trees were. I have a good eye. I saw foliage movement several times. I hoped you saw me when I showed myself on the edge of the forest. Though I snuck back in the cover of the trees, I saw you when you sneaked into the forest. I thought… so she takes the left circle and I take the right and we have to hook up somewhere."

"I guess you're right. Two heads are better than one. And we are two tough broads."

Three days later, the campground held a potluck celebration in the picnic pavilion. Every type of casserole, salad, fruit plate and dessert MG could imagine lay before her. Balloons, colorful table clothes and paper plates added to the festiveness.

Gladys sidled up to MG and stretched her hand in the direction of the table. "What do you think? We wanted a celebration in your honor."

Guilt crawled over MG. She had silently criticized all of Gladys' work. Yet she had been the one to single-handedly organize the gala event in her honor. MG attempted to hide the cloudiness in her eyes.

"Gladys, thank you for all you do for the campground and for this very special night. I appreciate you."

MG piled luscious foods on her plate and headed to the spot that Annika and Jesse had chosen.

She sat down with a sigh. "People come and go throughout the camping season. But of all the campers in this campground, you two will be the ones I will miss the most. Annika, we share a bond that will always live in my heart, no matter how far you travel."

Annika put her hand over MG's. "You are a special woman. I'll never forget you and our triumph to catch the bad guy."

"I guess, I chose the wrong day to go to town," said Jesse, "I should have been there to help you ladies out. Then again, with you two amazing women in control, you didn't need me."

"Thanks for your kind words, Jesse. I hope you both have safe travels and tons of adventures."

"I'm sure we will," said Annika. We want to see more of Colorado and then plan to fly to Sweden. I want Jesse and my dad to meet each other."

MG watched the couple leave the pavilion hand in hand. She was ready for calm and solitude. Well, kind of. Adventure suited her too.

Rueben pulled up a chair beside MG. "Thanks for your kind words to Gladys. She's been glowing ever since."

"Of course. She did a superb job putting this potluck together. Just look around at all the chatter and laughter."

"I picked up something for you at Ted's Place."

"I can't take any more glory. I don't need a thing."

"Well, here it is."

Rueben slid a fat newspaper in front of her. The front page was all Maggie with the headline:

Maggie Grant Curtails Mayhem at Campground

A smile lingered on her face. Hmm. Wonder what my ex will think when he reads the story.

THE RETRIEVAL OF SANITY

By Carol Alford

The crawl skyward toward our chimney is not without agony. I have not had my hip replaced, so the left hip ball slips in the socket, grinding and popping each time I push against the wooden shingles protecting our house, climbing higher and higher. We have the steepest roof in the neighborhood which means the winter snow slides off with the speed of a race car crossing the finish line. Although my slide might be the thrill of a-down-hill slalom, landing could end in a mass of jutting bones. Thus, my crawl is cautious and deliberate. But I'm on a mission.

Because of the Cape Cod structure, it's necessary to clamber close to the edge. I resist peering to the ground below. The left hand has acquired several splinters from the vise grip applied to the roof edge, but my conscious thought tries to deny this fact. I tow a rope attached to a sturdy milk crate my husband has saved for decades. In his past life he owned grocery stores, and they don't make crates like that anymore. So, the crate is to be my heroine. I've decided it's a she, like me.

Several clouds float by as I pull myself up to straddle the peak of the roof and then scoot to the smokestack. My fingers dig into the spaces between the chimney bricks, and I haul myself upright. It's a stretch to reach the gaping opening that tunnels to the living room fireplace below. I will my body to end its quivering and wave the crate to the heavens for balance. When stability ensues, my movements are slow motion as I wrench the crate in place. *S-c-r-u-u-n-n-c-h*. It is a welcome sound. *Nothing will enter the chimney again.*

Now, I like furry things and believe they should have equal freedom in this democracy we inhabit. But…Rigging up and dragging a garden hose with a high-pressure nozzle to eliminate the raccoon poop on the nearly vertical roof—like I've done for a few years—is not on my list of *tolerable outside chores for spring and summer.* I'm convinced that the paralyzing nightmares I endured during those years are the result of troubled sleep brought on by the romping raccoons.

You may sense that I am breathing easier this summer, and the nightmares, well, they have taken a less paralyzing form. All because of the revelation concerning the reason for the pooping and the romping.

Picture me prying the fireplace flue—now that's a tongue twister—open wide enough to accept a twisted arm. My hair is already sooty as I squat in the fireplace. At the end of my distorted arm, spidery fingers search for the writhing bodies inside. The screeching from their hungry mouths pierces like an ice pick. One by one, my fingers slither around each long belly. I feel like some contortionist as I pluck them from their den. Suspended, their spindly legs and clawed feet jut out as if to grip the air. Four pointy mouths work endlessly with each desperate screech. My senses cannot endure their discord. The ringed eyes and tail of their future coat is evident, yet I cannot see the beauty in their hairlessness.

I know that their mother is dead. When she was alive, they were fed each night. They were quiet, a mere whisper, like the breezes. *Then* I was not aware that the romping and pooping meant raccoon babies in the chimney. No more. Sanity prevails.

THE HUDDLING PLACE

By Carol Alford

Not unlike many of the farm homes during the forties, our wind-battered windows rattled, desperately trying to keep the outdoors out. Not entirely successful, if one looked closely, fine white frosty stuff filtered into a few corners behind the see-though curtains. The warmest spot was near the shiny, chocolate brown coal burner in the front room. It was a huddling place. We huddled at night as our PJ's, fetched from frozen bedrooms toasted. We huddled in the morning, leaving mountains of bed covers, icy linoleum and foggy cool breath in our sleeping rooms.

TJ, my sidekick younger brother and I huddled giggling at our melting nose-sickles as we stripped off soggy knitted mittens and hats. Bits of packed snow spit and hissed as they hit the coal burner when we shook our snowsuits. As Mom draped them near the huddling place, we knew they would lose their wetness by morning. Then Dad and Mom would let us bundle up and help with the after-breakfast chores, since we were not yet old enough to help milk the ten cows, which was a before breakfast chore.

The early morning glow of the winter sunrise bathed the kitchen wall in orangy gold. TJ and I chased around the kitchen table, knocking chairs askew. It was a blend of teamwork and competition when it came to setting the table.

"Settle down kids!" Mom's admonition accompanied a flash from her eyes as she looked up from the blackened cast iron skillet filled with sizzling pork side from the home grown and home butchered pig. We indeed settled down. TJ was in charge of the syrup and the butter stored in the pantry at the top of the cellar stairs while I worked meticulously skimming the risen cream from the milk crock and ladling the thickest part into the cream crock for butter churning, and the rest into Dad's cream pitcher.

"Here comes Dad," I say as I look up from my last dip into the milk crock. Tip, Dad's faithful wolf-like German Shepherd and Smoochie, the fluffy Collie that belongs to TJ and I trot alongside. The pooches curl up on the screened porch while dad sets the pail of the family's milk on the porch table and hangs up his milking clothes.

Inside he pours the rich warm milk into a freshly scrubbed crock to be refrigerated and skimmed tomorrow or the next day, pours steaming water from the teakettle which perpetually sits at the back of the coal cook stove and washes up at the kitchen sink. Mom already has four pancakes ready to be flipped on the griddle.

"Smells like pork side and buttermilk pancakes, and I'm really hungry," Dad says as he adjusts the farm news station on the kitchen wood-box radio.

As the last stack of golden cakes are placed on the table Mom asks, "John did I see you limping as you came in?"

"Yeah, I'm going to have to start hobbling the brindle. She really whopped me in the knee as I walked behind her and nearly stepped in the bucket three times while I was milking her." He sighs and places one fried egg smack dab on top of his stack of buttered and syruped pancakes.

"Mighty good breakfast Jackie," Dad says to Mom as TJ and I help clear the table. The farm news captures Dad's ear as we dry each dish then use the white painted kitchen chair to reach the high cupboard shelves. We want to be ready when Dad returns to the chores.

Sitting in Old Green, the GMC with the black fenders we feel the jarring each time a fork-full of steamy sour corn silage hits the truck bed as Dad forks it from the upright steel silo. A few times he let us help him tramp the freshly chopped corn as it was blown into the tall structure, but only when the silo was no more than half full. One time, TJ and I climbed the enclosed ladder of the upright steel silo—clear up to the top. I don't know if Dad knows.

White-faced cattle snort and crowd along the feed bin at the edge of the corral as Dad scoops out their morning meal, steaming in the biting air. Dad works fiercely to keep up with the driverless truck carrying two wide-eyed kids. Old Green is set in what Dad calls 'low-low', chug, chug, chugging beside the stretching feed trough. Before we reach the end Dad swings over the side of the truck bed and into the cab to press the squeaky brake for the stop.

TJ tromps 'long side Dad cutting his way through eight inches of glistening snow toward the cow corral where they check the water trough and carry hay from the barn. I join Mom at the granary where she is filling the grain buckets. Opening the wheat granary, I am as startled at the mouse that scurries to get out of the grain bin.

"Mom! Look! Mousie is here again," I shriek. He finally makes headway in the shifting grain and scampers out of sight. We giggle.

The laying hens squawk and cackle as we scatter the grains along the chicken feeders. The older queens of the chicken house peck the young pullets who try to crowd in, making them jump and flap their white feathered wings. We spread some extra straw around the smelly hen house and pump two buckets of water.

Following the path around the back of the chicken house Mom and I stop at the coal shed to replenish the coal buckets. Inside the dark space Mom breaks a large chunk by banging it with the shovel and fills a bucket for the kitchen cook stove and a bucket for the front room.

Afternoon finds TJ and I trudging out to our snow cave carved into a drifted-over ditch in front of the house. It is already four feet long. We clear a little newly drifted snow at the entrance and craw inside on all fours. It is too narrow for us to fit side by side, so I go first and dig out another foot or so with my mittened hands. Behind me, TJ pushes the newly dug snow out of the cave. Then we trade for the next twelve inches, all the while pretending that we are lost in a blizzard and are making a snow house for the winter. In our fantasy TJ goes hunting for food while I pat the snow to make a table at a wide part of our cave. Muffled yips come closer as I stop to listen. It's Smoochie covered with globs of snow hanging on her fury body who wiggles in ahead of TJ. She adds to the adventure of our make believe, but ruins part of the cave in her exuberant tail wagging, squirming, and face licking.

Darkness closes as the setting sun dips behind the hovering Rockies. With a five-foot lead, TJ says, "I'll beat you to the house." He doesn't beat me. Nearing the house, we smell something good which turns out to be chicken and noodles, mashed potatoes, home canned beans, and coleslaw.

"I get an egg." TJ had spotted a yolk floating with the noodles and grabs the noodle-serving spoon.

"Me too," I chime.

"Hey you two, hold on. There were several eggs in that old stewing hen when I dressed her and everyone can have one," Mom says as she retrieves the serving spoon. "Now wait for your dad to wash his hands."

After supper, we all huddle in the front room. The newspaper crackles as Dad, seated in a platform rocker cozied near the coal burner, shuffles through each page. Mom feeds the burner a loaf-pan-sized chunk of coal and sits at the end of the couch near her mending basket. She finishes a sock and slips an old light bulb into another. TJ and I stretch out on the well-worn rug in front of the dancing flames licking at the open designs of the stove door. Taking turns, we toss the dice and move the marbles around a homemade marble board. I win. He wins.

"Hey, will you play with us, Mom and Dad?" I ask.

"OK, just one more game and then to bed." It's Dad who answers.

We move red, blue, black, and yellow marbles around the board. The night wind whistles 'round us, yet there is a glowing coziness amidst gentle laughter as each of us tries for the best count with our roll of the dice. And Dad emerges the winner.

Remembering—eons later I still feel the warmth and security of this huddling place—in my bones, in my heart and in my soul. It has given me strength in life's awesome, but swift journey and continues to carry me into each new challenge and adventure.

AREA CODE 970

By Carol Alford

Fall–2009

Gosh what would it be—adventure, romance, mystery, discovery, disappointment? It would take four hours to get to the spot she circled on the Wyoming map. Her youngest son, Sean, knew where she was going and why. She remembered his crooked grin, like her own, when he said, "Well, all I can say is you were never afraid of a risk. You're a gutsy lady and I hope you have three fabulous days. Love ya, Mom." Was she gutsy? Maybe. Or—maybe just crawling out of her shell. Or—getting new wings. Cricket Jameson, feeling more youthful than her forty-eight years, shifted the silver bullet, as she called it into the overdrive fifth gear and felt the smooth glide of her tidy little Nissan truck. The matching silver truck-bed topper enclosed the multi-colored tapestry bag, fat with carefully chosen items for her three days stay.

Humming in duet with the radio, she found herself singing the last few lines.

> *Tell me you love me for a million years*
> *And if it don't work out*
> *And if it don't work out*
> *You'll have to tell me goodbye*

It had worked out with Jack for twenty-five years. Not that Jack Jameson was an easy man to live with. She was one thousand percent sure of his loyalty and faithfulness. However, living with Jack could be lonely—sometimes even when he was in the same room. She knew that other cops' wives felt the same. Fence posts whipped by as she momentarily closed her eyes, sucked in and blew out a full breath, remembering. *Oh, where did those three years go?*

Spring–2006

"I'm sorry Cricket. No more treatment. We just had to close him up." Cricket waved away the medicinal hospital smell that overcame her and compounded her sense of dread. "What can we do now Allen?" He had been the family doctor for so long that she never called him Dr. Perkins. "Jack's suffered so much through eight months of chemo. He hasn't kept any food down for over a week." "Take him home. You can do as much for him as we can. Love him and hold him. Call Hospice to help with his home care and pain killers." But he never went home. He ignored her pleas. "Honey, please come home. We can be together. You'll have everything you need. You'll be comfortable. Look at me Jack." His hand felt bony and limp, but she refused to let go as he pulled away, eyes riveted to the drawn shades, that blocked out the spring sunshine and gave the hospital room an eeriness. "I told you Cricket, my life is over. I'm outta here. Forget me. I don't want you or anyone watching this crap." His tube-laden arm crashed against the soft blanket. "Come off this pity party, Jack. It's not easy for any of us. None of us asked for this. We're not ready to lose you. Let me take you home." "I told you I'm already gone. Now get the hell out of here. Let me go." Refusing to let the harshness of his voice cut her, she softened and pleaded, "Ben's coming home tomorrow. His commander gave him two weeks leave, just to be with you. Please. I want us all to be together. To share old times." "It'll be a wasted trip for Ben. I don't want him here. I said goodbye at Christmas." "Well, both of your sons want to be with you. You can't keep them away." "The hell I can't. I'll have the door locked." Cricket's phone vibrated in her jeans pocket. The buzzing and tickling had stopped by the time she palmed her phone. *What now? A call from work.* Cricket glared at her husband, pivoted and stomped out of the room. Cricket managed the largest and busiest service station owned by self-made millionaire, Bill Cooper. It included a wide selection of foods and beverages in the convenience store, a three-bay car wash and fully automated gas, diesel, and propane service. Ten years ago, it had not been the busiest and best run complex in Northern Colorado, but her hard work and willingness to take a risk had paid off for the Cooper family and for Cricket. The business almost ran itself from a manager's point of view these days and usually she didn't have to put in overtime hours. Not this week, however. She'd lost two of her part-time employees. James said he would take on extra shifts until Cricket could hire new people. Then, the new computer went down. Everything, including the pumps shut off when that happened. She had worked out a back-up system until the computer specialist could arrive tomorrow to correct the glitches in the new system. *Now what?* Cricket gritted her teeth and dialed her work number. "Coopers. Jenny speaking." "Jenny. This is Cricket. What's up?" "Hate to spring this on you. James didn't show up for work. I have a class in thirty minutes. A final. I can't miss it." "Holy cow. I'll be right there. I'm at the hospital, so it should take me less than fifteen minutes." Her husband's image evaporated from her mind for the moment as she fumbled with the keys and unlocked Jack's Bronco. The Bronco shuddered, clanged, and rattled as she banged over the hospital speed bumps without slowing. Jack needs to get rid of this old bucket of bolts, she thought. But she knew this was one of the many decisions she would make alone. *Hold on Cricket. You can't fall apart.* Only eight minutes and she burst into Coopers and heard the update from Jenny. "Well, I found out what happened to James. That new horse he's been working with threw him into a pile of rocks. His leg's broken pretty bad and he's in emergency surgery." Cricket's shoulders slumped as she stammered, "Bummer. One of my best workers." "Sorry I had to bother you." "That's my job Jenny." Cricket shooed her with a flick of her hand. "Be off. Call me in the morn after 7:00. I'll need to reschedule. Maybe you can take an extra shift before you head out for spring break." Four patrons were lined up at the counter when she slipped behind it. Cricket rarely worked the counter—only in emergencies. It looked like this would be a whole week of emergencies. Tomorrow Ben, her oldest son, would arrive. Her assistant manager was lying somewhere with a broken leg—in surgery—Jenny had said. She had a help wanted sign in the window and ads in the newspaper. When she got applications, there would be interviews. Keeping reliable help was not an easy task. In the meantime, she would work the counter, put in extra hours to sort and count the money, do the books, reports, orders and bank deposits. It would be a late night and back in the morning before 6:00. Conflicted between managerial responsibilities and her dying husband, who didn't want her near him, her stomach tightened. *Stop it Cricket. Get a move on.* Cricket braced the phone between her ear and shoulder as she worked with customers at the wide front desk. She dialed Sean and heard the fifth ring before he answered. "Sean, it's Mom. Emergency at work." She turned to help the customer. "Slide your card here, please. Thank you." Speaking to Sean again, "What's your schedule tomorrow? Can you pick up Ben from the airport? He comes in at 2:10 in the afternoon. You'd need to leave town before 1:00." "Sure Mom. I'm finished with classes at noon. I'll work on my econ project tomorrow night. Can't wait to talk to Ben. Maybe we can figure someway to change Dad's mind about coming home." Cricket's eyes filled thinking of her sons. Sean would earn his two-year business credential from Front Range at the end of the year. Then maybe to Colorado State. Ben, as young as he was, used his mechanical skills on some of the Air Force's most exotic jets. She and Jack had raised two responsible and loving sons. A sigh escaped her lips. All afternoon Cricket maneuvered from task to task without much thought. The back-up computer system couldn't keep up with the steady flow of customers and she didn't leave the counter until she shut the doors at 11:00 p.m. It was close to midnight before she stepped into the spring night and dragged each foot to the Bronco. At home, drained and discouraged, she pressed the play button on the answering machine. Her father, traveling with his new wife, called from Canada wanting to know how Jack was. He would call another time. The other call was from Jack's partner on the force who also played in the softball league with Jack. "Cricket, it's Tom. I heard things are bad for Jack. Is there anything I can do for either of you? I gotta do something! Let me know. OK?" *Too late to call Tom.* Somehow, she'd work in a call tomorrow and ask if Tom could get some of the police staff and ball players to drop by the hospital during the week—anything to help Jack feel alive, a real person who mattered. Jack would be furious if he knew, but she believed he'd never be nasty with the guys. She couldn't allow him to spend his last days alone. Her mind whirled as she pulled her night shirt over her head and imagined Jack in his hospital room staring into nothing. Crawling between the sheets, she sensed her own emptiness crawl from her toes and slither over every part of her body. Throughout their marriage, they spent few nights apart. She would never again feel the warmth of his closeness, never reach over to stroke his arm or his furry chest. Even when he treated her with frostiness, he always said, "Night Crick. Love ya." Never again. Why was he so adamant about not coming home? Glaring into the black ceiling, tears trickled into her ears. Again. She hated that and flopped over, burying her face into the pillow. In the morning…And she drifted away. Nearing dawn she found herself in a maze, running through one opening and then another. She had to find Jack, but her feet, heavily laden, moved in slow motion. There he was at the end of the corridor. When she reached for his outstretched hands, she found nothing but a pile of smelly rags. Far away she heard tinkling grow louder and louder until her awareness of the wrenching dream welcomed the beckoning of the alarm clock. "Oh Lord. It's morning. Help me through this day."

⸻ ◆ ⸻

She made it through the day. Jenny came to her rescue by cancelling her spring break skiing trip. "I'm not all that excited about skiing," said Jenny. "The last time I nearly broke my neck. Being here at work will save me a bunch of money." "Oh, Jenny. You're an angel. Can I adopt you? I'd love to have a daughter." During the next evening—Ben's second day home—Cricket rolled tortillas around the green chili, pork and bean mixture that was one of her specialties. As Ben set the table for the two of them, she smothered the burrito with extra green chili, heaped sharp cheddar on top and added shredded lettuce and diced tomatoes. "I didn't think I was hungry, but it smells mighty good, Mom. And I see you made fresh salsa on the side. Yum." Cricket gave him a lop-sided grin as Ben continued. "I know you want Dad home with us, but I get him. He can't take it. Us watching him in pain, watching him die. Too many memories here to face." "Augh," Cricket growled to the air. "I guess you know him better than I do." "We had a good visit this afternoon, even if it was a short one. He tires pretty fast. Then he gets to slurring his words. That embarrasses him." "Well, he won't talk to me. He seems mad all the time. And there is so much I want to say, before it's too late." "Oh, Mom. That's *his* hurt. He's thinking of the years he'll miss being with you. Dad's tough on the outside but feels way deeper than you could ever imagine. He said something about chasing you away all the time and he's sorry about that. Said you are the best thing that ever happened to him." Cricket returned a forked bite of burrito back onto her plate. She rested her hands on the table edge and made no attempt to prevent the tears that plopped into her lap. Silence floated between them. Once she regained her composure, Cricket spoke. "He said that?"

"He did. There's still time Mom. What do you want to say?" "I want to tell him how important he is to me, how much I love him, that I still need his input in this partnership. Darn it, I want his advice." "About what, Mom?" "I don't know if I can say it…How to use the life insurance money. I want to be prepared, maybe buy my own business. How can I ask him? I don't want him to think I'm waiting for him to die. But I need him. Need his opinions." Ben stood and placed his hands on her shoulders, then leaned to kiss the top of her head. "Talk to him. Let me clean up. You go. Now." When Cricket tip-toed into Jack's room, she saw a glow from the TV. A ballgame, but with no sound. Jack's eyes flickered as she stepped to his bedside. No smile yet. "What ya doing here?" he asked. Cricket hoped the gruffy sound of his voice stemmed from hoarseness, not anger. She fingered a lock of his hair and allowed her hand to slide down his cheek, roughened with bearded stubble.

"Came to keep you company." She noticed a hint of a smile creep into the corners of his mouth. "Don't think I've had enough company today, huh?" She knew Tom hoped to get some of the ball team together to visit. She wondered if it worked out. "I know Ben came by. Sean, too, after his class. Any others?" "Well, Crick…" A sigh escaped his lips. "I suppose you sent Tom and the guys over." "I didn't send them, but…"

"Well, they came. Five of them." Jack waved a hand toward the small family bed wedged against the wall. An orange softball jersey with the number11 in white blocks stretched across the bed. Jack always wore the number 11, but everyone called the number double ones. They said he was a number one batter and a number one third baseman. "Oh my. Oh my." Cricket grabbed the jersey and placed it over Jack's chest and stepped back to gaze at her husband. "Indeed, you are, and always were double ones—on the force, on the ball field and at home." Her tears blurred everything in front of her, but she saw Jack's hand reach toward hers. For the next half an hour she sat beside Jack, their hands entwined. Jack told her about the supper-time visit, that the team would hang double ones in the dugout at every game for luck, that the guys even snuck in a beer for Jack to have a few swigs, and that it felt good to laugh. Cricket talked about James and his broken leg, and Jenny's thoughtfulness in giving up her spring break trip. They talked about their sons, Ben, and Sean. Jack moaned, and his eyes closed. "Do you need some more morphine?" Jack swallowed and shook his head. "I can pump it in whenever I want to." Cricket listened to his labored breathing knowing there was nothing she could do. She needed to let him rest. Cricket kissed Jack's mouth and winced at his breath, like rotting potatoes. "Goodnight, honey. See you tomorrow," she whispered. The following day flew by in a whirl. The stars were in her favor, at least partly. Cricket hired two new employees—one full time and one part time. Jenny would help with some of the training. Anxious to spend time with Jack, she left the service station at 5:30. Arriving at Jack's room, she sat on the side chair while two nurses hovered over her husband. One checked his blood pressure and temperature while the other emptied the bag attached to his catheter. "Are you planning to stay for dinner?" asked the catheter nurse. Cricket eyed her husband, searching his reaction. He shrugged his shoulders toward her. "Yes, I'm staying," she said. When the nurses left, Cricket noticed a giant, and colorfully decorated, homemade card propped on the air unit. "Any more visitors today?" "Tom came by. Brought that card over there from work. Lots of messages. Some clever, and others... um touching." "Nice. Any more beer today?" "Naw. Doesn't taste like I remember anyway. I hear the food cart coming. I'm not hungry, but why don't you get something from the cafeteria?" She returned from the food court with a green salad, brownie, and milk. Jack's gelatin, applesauce, milk, and saltines looked sparse on his tray. Cricket emptied the crouton package onto her salad and began eating. She wanted to say. "Jack, try a few bites. You need to eat something." She didn't. She didn't bring up the insurance money either. Instead, Cricket remembered the past. "I wish Carrie and her husband hadn't moved to Kentucky. I miss her. It's because of her, you asked me out." Carrie and Cricket were best friends clear through high school, just as Jack, Tom and Carrie's older brother were best buds. Jack stifled a yawn and gathered strength to speak. "Yeah, I wouldn't have paid much attention to you—you were a pain in the ass—if Carrie hadn't dared you to dive off the rocks at the reservoir." Jack sighed. "You nearly drowned, and I had to save you." "I have a confession to make. I wasn't drowning. I pretended to be in trouble, so you could save me."

"That was downright sneaky." "It worked, didn't it? Well, it took a while for you to really notice me, not until I graduated high school, and you were at the police academy." "Looking back, I have some re..." Jack coughed and turned to the side. Then he couldn't stop coughing. Cricket started for the door to get a nurse, but Jack yelled out, "No, just need..." He pointed to the tissues. Cricket pulled a handful from the box and held them to his mouth. He closed his eyes and spit until all the globs of blood were cleared from his throat. "Didn't want you to see that." "Oh, honey, it hurts me that you're suffering, but please don't push me away. Every moment with you is precious. Don't you know that?" Jack sipped some water and asked Cricket to lower the head of the bed. He then patted the spot next to him. Cricket eased herself to his side and they looked into each other's eyes. Jack's lips parted. "I'm sorry I've been rough to live with. I took the troubles of my job home instead of leaving them on the streets. I had to be tough. You got the brunt of that." Cricket pressed her finger against his lips to shush him. "We aren't robots. Frustrations, disappointments, pressures bring all kinds of turmoil and crazy feelings. We have to live life. And you've done that. And you've been my partner all the way." They drifted into their own thoughts, in their own quietness, feeling the closeness of each other. Jack's eyes glistened when he spoke once more. "We made amazing sons, didn't we?" "Absolutely." She couldn't stop nodding. "And I know in my bones, they'll live their lives as a tribute to their father." Another quiet moment passed. Jack squeezed his wife's hand. "Well, Crick, I hear you're thinking of owning your own business." Cricket's mouth fell open. "You know about the lube business for sale?" "You know you can't put anything past me in this partnership." Jack took a heavy breath and pushed on. "Nothing better than a well-established, family-owned business with a reliable following. They always treated us well. I know you'll carry on the tradition." "You don't think I'm crazy to go it alone?" "Hell no…Not my wife with the crackerjack business mind." Night closed around the couple. Cricket turned to her other side, and they lay cupped together. Cricket felt Jack's arm, as weak as it was, draw her close as he said, "Don't look back, Crick. Go for it. Night Crick." She grinned. Sometime after she left, he died. Alone. Cricket believed it was with his own dignity. Cricket and her sons held a simple memorial in the mortuary chapel. Most of the police force and half the town crowded in to remember Jack Jameson. Ben and Sean reminded her of different aspects of their father as they rose to speak. In Ben she heard Jack's voice and remembered his deep-set eyes and heavy dark brows. Sean had his dad's healthy build, the same broad shoulders, and head pose. More importantly, she sensed Jack's gifts of strength, perseverance, and loyalty in her sons. An era slipped away from Cricket, Ben and Sean, but they would carry Jack with them forever.

Late summer 2009

Cricket's Lube and Service kept Cricket hopping as the months turned into years, more than three years, in fact. Jack was right. She had a good head for business and the risk had been worth it. Completing his Associates Business degree, Sean became her right hand as the business took hold. It was 6:30 p.m. Saturday. Alone, and the last one to leave, she swung the hinged cabinet over the secret floor safe where the money bags lay until Monday morning. She could sure use one of Jack's back and neck massages right now, and smiled thinking of him. She leaned back against the smooth leather of her swivel chair. Tingles crept from her slender thighs to her toes as she stretched her booted feet in front of her. Cricket tucked rust-colored wisps that had escaped her ponytail behind her ears and rotated her shoulders to loosen them. Maybe she should straighten her desk and work on the accounts to get a head start on Monday's business. Anything to put off the emptiness of Saturday night. Through her office door, she watched reflections from the endless traffic slide across the wide panes of tinted glass in the reception area. A brief hum in the back of her throat punctuated her heavy sigh. Everyone but me has a place to go, a place to be, she thought. Unless she wanted to keep spending her weekends alone, she'd better say yes, the next time Tony or Jeff or Thomas asked her out. Yet, she shivered at the image of dating and going through the awkwardness of being with a man she hardly knew. At times she planned something for the weekend. There had been movies, dinner at a favorite restaurant, and plays. Sometimes with one of her married friends, but more often alone. At least half of the time she spent the evening lying in bed surrounded by crackers, cheese and apple slices clicking the remote trying to find something desirous on TV. Oh heck, she didn't feel like pulling up the account on the computer and she wasn't compulsive about a neat desk. Her eyelids closed in the darkness and her mind went into slow motion. The calm stretched on. Cricket's relaxed body jerked and stiffened to the piercing shrillness interrupting her solitude. Clawing through a foggy thickness, her fingers reached out. The sound ended when she knocked the phone into the oak desk organizer, scattering paper clips, pens and pencils.

Her hand finally made a successful grab, but her voice failed her the first time. Instead of the usual business greeting, she spewed, "Hello?" "Ginger is that you? Did I catch ya sleepin' or somethin'?" His voice had a smile in it and a resonance that almost echoed. Barely getting her bearings, she shook her head to the din that lingered there. "What? Well, I guess you did catch me nodding off, but we don't have a Ginger here." "Well, I'll be horn swoggled. My call didn't make it to my sis in Georgia, then?" "I'm afraid not. You got Colorado. Sorry." "Can you figure that? I'm calling from Wyoming. Do you suppose I punched the wrong key? Sometimes I'm all thumbs." This was ridiculous continuing such an unlikely conversation. But she did not hang up. "What area code did you dial?" "Gosh, I don't remember. Let me see. Oh, yeah. Well, it was either 770 or 970. My writing's a little scribbly. Sometimes I can't tell my nines from my sevens." "Guess you dialed 970 and got me. Try 770 next time. I hope you reach your sister all right." The sound of her own words tinkled in her ears. "Well, at least tell me a little about this mystery lady I'm talkin' to in Colorado. Your voice has me pretty intrigued." She admonished herself. Hang up. Hang up. Just because you are alone on Saturday night does not mean that you should talk to some compete stranger. This is asinine. But she didn't hang up. "Oh, it does, does it? There's not much to tell. I own a lube and auto service business. I'm a widow with two grown sons. What about you?" "I'm a bachelor who loves these here Wyoming hills and I've tromped a many of them—huntin', fishin', fixin' fence or brandin' on the McDonald ranch over the hill from me. Just retired after twenty-five years at the refinery near Bar Oil, so now I have more time for tromping and 4-wheeling." And on went the banter. Laughing at a hunting fiasco Charlie described, Cricket's eye caught the hands of the wall clock—9:00. They had rattled on more than two hours and she hadn't felt so giddy in eons. "Charlie, I really need to go home. These peanut butter and cheese crackers I'm chewing on are just making my stomach growl." "Well, all I can say, Miss Cricket is that I've never had a more enjoyable Saturday night. You are a great talkin' lady. I have this feelin' this call was supposed to happen. Can we talk again? How about it?" Biting on her lip, Cricket searched for a response. "I don't know Charlie…it's just…" "Tell you what. You call the shots. Take my phone number and think about it. Then when you're ready for another visit, you can call me. What do ya say?" Feeling foolish a few minutes later, she folded the blue sheet from her desk pad, scribbled with a phone number, stuck it behind the bank card in her billfold and picked up her car keys. Rolling her eyes at herself, she steered through the weekend traffic. He sounded like he had a great passion for life, for the mountains and people. But what could one tell from a random phone call? It would be silly to call him. She wouldn't.

Temptation and curiosity twisted and tugged at her. One day Cricket was dead sure about the absurdity of pursuing this contact and the next day she could not get the whole thing out of her head. Remembering the friendliness of his voice, she wondered whether he was disappointed that she hadn't called. Cricket fingered the numbered blue slip of paper and picked up the phone only to bang it into its cradle at her own silliness. Two weeks after the chance phone call, Cricket's impulsive nature won.

"Cricket, it's really you. Wow! Hearing your voice again makes my day. Start talkin' mystery lady. I want to hear all about the last two weeks."

She heard the grin in his voice. "Not much to tell. The lube and service business keeps me busy. We have customers lined up most of the day. Course my son, Sean manages and trains all the technicians."

"You two must make a good team. I like gettin' under the hood and makin' an engine purr myself. Gotta keep these vehicles runnin' and good for the road."

"So, you're a good mechanic then?"

"Well. I'd say I can hold my own against a goodly lot. Worked on a bunch of machinery over at Bar Oil in the refinery. Even do perdy good with the new electronics."

"How'd you learn about them?"

"Took a class at the community college. Like to learn new things and like to work with my hands."

Cricket sighed and shook her head. "I can see it now, you whittling out a fancy arrow to use hunting. You said you're a good hunter." Cricket grinned to herself imagining deft hands at work."

"You got it. I do some whittlin'. Haven't done any bow hunting yet. But maybe next year. Now, Miss Cricket, tell me how Ben's doing."

"You have a good memory, Charlie. I can't believe you remember my oldest son's name."

"Not only do I remember his name, but I remember he's an Air Force mechanic, but I don't know where he's working."

"You're something else. Ben's near Goldsboro at Seymour Johnson Air force Base."

"Oh yeah, I read about those F-15s they have there. In North Carolina, right?"

Talking to Charlie removed the mundane of the day-to-day. Even tasks of hiring and training new personnel, confronting a shoplifter or whipping up a batch of orange marmalade sounded fascinating as she heard her own blow by blow tales.

"Miss Cricket, it does my heart good to hear such passion for your work an' just life in general. As I look out this here westerly winder, some blustery clouds are turnin' crimson as the sun's headin' out toward sleep. And between them clouds are slivers of bright turquoise. Sure like ta be seein' such a sight with you."

Charlie and Cricket racked up many hours on the phone the next few weeks—chewin' the fat as Charlie called it. It was a fresh breath for Cricket, invigorating each day and freeing her from the heaviness of being alone, without Jack. She looked forward to hearing his cheerful voice.

"Mystery lady."

"I'm not a mystery lady Charlie. I've told you just about everything there is to know about me."

"Yeah, but until yur standin' right here in front of my brown eyes, you'll have to be my mystery lady. Wishin' that could happen. Are ya up to it?"

"I don't know Charlie."

"Don't ya think Sean could look out for things for a few days? From what you been sayin' you haven't had a break since you hung that shingle out front. Right?"

Cricket heard his insistent tone as her eyes locked on Jack's chair. It blurred in front of her. She sucked in air that whistled across her teeth. *Let go of Jack. He's gone.*

"Cricket?"

"Let me think about it. OK?"

Cricket sat on the idea of driving to Wyoming to meet Charlie for a couple of days. She'd always had good instincts about people and as a cop's wife she learned self-defense and believed she could handle any situation. She had no reason to suspect Charlie had anything to hide or that meeting him would be unsafe. Still, as a single woman, she wanted to be wise. She'd call Tom.

Cricket snugged against the smooth black leather of the corner booth at *Paul's Burgers and Stuff* and watched the amusement in Tom's eyes as she told him about the accidental phone call and the invitation.

"Tom, as Jack's friend and mine. As a police officer, I want your input."

"How can I help?"

"I believe Charlie's a good man and I'm curious to meet him in person. Could you check him out for me?"

Tom shrugged. "Sure. Give me what you know about the guy, and I'll get to it tomorrow." Cricket heard Tom's pen scratch against the note pad as she clicked off all she knew about Charlie.

"You say he took class at a community college. Know which one?"

Cricket shook her head. "Why? Would that help?"

"Guess we'd know he tells the truth if there's a record there. I have enough to get started. I'll do what I can and get back to you."

Two days later Cricket and Tom sat in the same booth at *Paul's Burgers and Stuff*. Tom shoved a folder across the table. Cricket's stare fixed on the folder and then at Tom.

"Open it. It won't bite."

Cricket clicked her tongue at him and licked her lips. "I...Well. Ok. She pulled a fistful of sheets from the folder. "Looks like you were quite thorough. What's in here?"

"You can read it all when you get home, but your friend Charlie has nothing to hide. No arrests, no driving tickets, no bankruptcies, a good employment record and yes, he took classes at the community college campus at Rock Springs. That was a pretty good drive from his place up closer to Lander. And yes, his sister Ginger lives in Georgia. He's been in Wyoming all his life. His parents died in a plane crash near Jackson about 15 years ago."

"Yeah. His dad was an auctioneer and took Charlie's mom with him to work a ranch sale. Bad weather." Cricket leaned back in her seat and gazed out the window. She sighed and nodded toward Tom. "Thanks."

Later that evening Sean poked his head inside Cricket's front door. "Hey mom, I'm here. Now what's all this stuff you need to talk about?"

"In the kitchen. Come on in. Just pulling a pizza from the oven."

"Oh, oh. I detect some bribery here. What job do you have for me?"

Cricket cut a wedge from the pizza, sizzling with Italian sausage, pepperoni, mushrooms, jalapeno slices and mozzarella, over a well-seasoned tomato sauce, and plopped it on Sean's plate. "Mostly I want your opinion. Then, maybe I have a job for you."

Sean blew on the corner of the pizza and then squinted up at his mom. "You're going to meet up with that Charlie guy and want me to hold down the fort while you're in Wyoming ... I just knew it."

Cricket rolled her eyes and shook her head fiercely. Her voice came out strong. "How'd you know?"

"Hold on Mom. You're a tough woman, but us guys need to keep an eye out. Don't want any bad to come to you. Tom called. I know he checked Charlie out. He showed me the reports."

"What? Can't believe he'd rat on me."

"It's not ratting on you. He cares."

"I know." Cricket lowered her eyes. Quiet lingered between them before she spoke again. "Shall I go?"

"Hey, that's your decision. But I'll support it if you do. You need some spice in your life. An adventure, a good time ... Maybe this is it." Sean stood and grabbed his mom in a bear hug. "I love you, Mom."

The following day Cricket made the call. After the usual *hellos, good to hear your voice, and how's it going?* parts of the phone conversation, a lull took over. Then, the force of Cricket's exhale sounded into the mouthpiece and her voice came alive. "Yes, Charlie, I think this is a good time to get away. How about next weekend?"

Fall 2009

Cricket enjoyed the changing Wyoming landscape as roads wound through drying grasslands dotted with bunches of sagebrush, an occasional patch of well-irrigated green meadow, and rocky peaks jutting skyward. Her mind wandered as she replayed the last several years of her life and contemplated this impulsive journey.

The static of the fading radio station brought Cricket's focus back to the present. She eyed the digital numbers indicating 11:15 and pressed the radio scanner button. Kenny Rogers' *Lady* played. It came in clear. *Damn. Turn right at the fork in the road, the one with the archway of pine. Missed it.*

She braked, and the silver Nissan skidded to a stop. Backing around to make the turn, the truck tires crunched on the gravel roadbed. Cricket lowered the window to let in the enticing mountain scent and took in a deep breath. *Hmm. Pine with a hint of spice.* She checked the odometer to clock the last seven miles to Charlie's place.

Skirted by mountains on each side, the road followed the twisting, nearly dry riverbed. Quite suddenly, she left the skyward steeples, plunging into barrenness—well not quite barren, with scratchy-looking tangles of sagebrush buried in powdery earth.

She squinted against the midday rays bouncing into her eyes and blinked to clear the rust-colored dust that billowed around her truck and swirled in through her open windows. Her furrowed brow hinted at the tightness building in her gut. Tingles pricked the edges of her skin and generated a full body shiver. One more mile and she should turn onto Charlie's lane.

"He said the lane winds back two miles," She blurted out loud.

Cricket's mind whirled, her heart pounded in her ears. *Boy, it seems desolate. And Charlie needs to work on that crumbling fence.*

Oh dear, is this a mistake? What am I doing in such woebegone country? Now Cricket, calm down, no cold feet. You've come this far. If he's a jerk, you can go home. But he's never sounded like a jerk. What's the worst that can happen?

She didn't let herself imagine what the worst could be. After all, she could handle anything. Right?

The last five minutes could have been an hour, like watching a slowed version of herself on video. So much so that a sharp right turn felt like steering through molasses. The abruptness of the road's end brought Cricket's eyes riveting. *There she is. Charlie's place.*

Staring at Cricket was a colorless single-wide modular. The modular's skirting gaped here and there, and gave the illusion of being toothless, while the faded awnings shading a pair of windows, made her look sleepy. A single pine, even in its scrubbiness, lent dignity to her.

Easing over the ruddy soil, she stopped in front of the scrubby pine. Her sigh wooshed in unison with the swishing truck door as she pushed it open. Cricket glanced up and caught a shadow behind the dark screen door.

When the door burst open, two lanky legs seemed to unfold into the daylight. Jutting elbows and knees vaulted from the porch landing, giving the illusion of a grasshopper.

"Here she is, my mystery lady. I've 'bout worn a path in the linoleum waitin'—and hopin' you didn't have trouble."

The jovial voice was familiar, and the ear-to-ear grin was warmly welcoming. Stunned, Cricket stepped from her truck. Before she found good footing, Charlie caught her hand in a bear-like grip and pumped it liberally.

"Howdy Miss Cricket. Man is it good to see you. And do you outshine the beauty of this countryside."

"Hi Charlie. I, I…"

Before she was able to speak another word, Charlie whisked her into the air and twirled twice as her feet floated. Her face brushed his cheek, and she detected a hint of a soapy scent. Gently landing her aground, his watchband caught her hair clasp, loosening the soft bronze ringlets that had been captured at the crown of her head.

"Wouldn't you know it? Me and my clumsiness! Well, ya look even prettier. How 'bout some grub? I bet you're hungry since it's about noontime."

Cricket finally found her voice as she grabbed her purse from the front seat. "Sure. I'm hungry, but I'd like to freshen up a little first."

Inside, once Cricket's eyes adjusted to leaving the sunlight; they scanned the simple, yet somewhat cluttered interior. A blue and gray plaid sofa appeared to be one that made into a bed. *I wonder if that's where I am to sleep.*

Across from the sofa sat a gold overstuffed armchair. Beside it stood an expansive end table made of knotty pine, littered with books three or four deep—both hard and soft cover—and an empty platter-sized ash tray. A bookcase took up one end of the room and held—rather haphazardly—magazines, pictures, more books, assorted candles, bowling trophies and a small TV. A well-worn leather recliner, its arms and head rest covered with faded yellow print terrycloth hand towels, angled against one corner of the bookcase.

At the opposite end of the room, the brown trampled rug ended, and the kitchen's yellow and brown linoleum began. Copper-colored canisters with black lids stood like soldiers between the sink and the stove on the nubby brown counter. To the left of the sink a mug tree held six he-man-sized cups of various colors and designs. A cheery yellow checkered oil cloth stretched across the wooden kitchen table sitting in the center of the room. The table was clear, except for a matching chunky pair of milk glass salt and pepper shakers and a wrought iron napkin holder stuffed with yellow paper napkins. Completing the kitchen area, two clunky wooden chairs flanked the ends of the table.

A side hall beyond the kitchen led to the bathroom where Cricket was glad to splash tepid water on her face, renew her coral lipstick and fix the smudged teal eye shadow which always brought out the green in her blue green eyes. She fiddled with her hair until it was secured in the hair clasp. Catching that soapy scent again, she realized it came from a squatty shaving mug and jutting lather brush still foamy. The sage green toothbrush holder held a purple toothbrush and plastic tumbler.

Cricket grinned at the green and lavender shower curtain, which emitted a new plastic scent and bared both vertical and horizontal fold markings. Brand new purple towels, too. That wasn't all. A tall glass filled with purple and yellow wildflowers proudly perched on the lid of the water closet. *He's certainly trying to make a favorable impression.*

"I hope yor 'bout spruced up, 'cause in two shakes of a lamb's tail our grub will be ready." Charlie's voice came from the kitchen. "I hope you like burgers and beans. Actually, it's ground venison, from the four point I bagged last huntin' season."

Stepping into the kitchen, Cricket said, "Burgers and beans sound fine. Those wildflowers are lovely. What a sweet touch. Did you find them nearby?'

"It's been pretty dry here on my little patch, but down the hill about a half mile is a meadow on Jake's place. That's where I found your posies. When I bought these three acres from Jake years ago, I chose this spot for the view, since I like feelin' like I'm on top of the world. Now sit yourself down while I pour our iced tea."

Charlie pulled a gallon jug from the refrigerator and filled glasses that seemed a foot tall. Charlie had set the table with dinner plates, flatware, bottles of steak sauce, catsup, relish, sliced dills and mustard, plus a platter of thickly sliced tomatoes and onions. Cricket heard the sizzling in the black iron skillet, covered with a lid twice its size, and sensed a whiff of the pork and beans, bubbling away in a small saucepan.

"What a spread you laid out Charlie. Everything looks and smells great."

"Miss Cricket, it's almost ready." Charlie speared four thick patties and tucked them into large buns and placed the filled plate on the already crowded table. He ladled beans from the pan onto her plate. "Now you tell me when to stop."

"No more. Enough beans. Thank you." Cricket lifted a venison burger from the plate, stacked it with onion and tomato, and slathered the bun with mustard and catsup. "I don't know if I'll be able to get my mouth around this burger."

Over the meal Cricket regarded Charlie more closely. She wondered how he could keep his lengthy rail-thin build, as he wolfed down two burgers and an extra venison patty. He had a pleasant face, with a wide forehead topped by a tuft of dark hair that kept the dome of his head from being completely bald. Charlie's smile showed off deep dimples.

However, his dark mustache that twitched when he talked, his long jaw, pointed chin and protruding left ear, gave him a comical look. One minute his dark snapping eyes appeared amused, and the next serious, and even wary. An interesting person, she thought.

They talked about her trip to Wyoming. He told her about shooting the deer, butchering, and how to make good venison burgers. When they finished the meal, Cricket helped put the condiments away while Charlie washed the dishes, skillet, and pot. Once he put them to drain on a towel next to the sink, he turned to her and said, "Let's go out and sit on the stoop while I have a smoke and I'll tell ya what I planned for your stay."

On the front steps, Cricket wrapped her arms around the legs of her brushed black denim jeans and rested her chin on her knees. She took in the majestic view. Charlie was right, looking west she could see for miles. In the distance, snowy peaks contrasted to the muted violet blue in the closer mountain ranges.

Charlie sprawled sideways beside her, leaning against an unpainted railing and blew streams of smoke overhead. "Ya know, it seems like the world is near perfect right about now. Just look at all this splendor." Charlie stretched his arm out in acknowledgement of the stunning panorama. "And you brought an extra ray of sunshine to my life."

Cricket smiled. "I don't know what to say. You've been so welcoming and thoughtful."

"You don't have to say a thing. I want you to feel relaxed, away from all your hustle and bustle. And I want you to have an adventure here—maybe like it so much, you'll want to come back time and time again. This is a powerful place, you know. Wyoming."

"That's what Sean said—to have an adventure and a good time. So, what about these plans you wanted to tell me about?"

"Tonight, I'm takin' you bowling over at the Knotty Pine. It's about 30 miles north of here. They serve great fish and chips and it's usually hoppin' on Friday night. Then tomorrow I'll show ya a secret little stream where we can catch Brookies till the cows come home. You can help me throw together a tater salad in the morning and we'll toss in some wieners to roast when we get hungry. And I thought we'd throw in my air mattress and tarp and sleep under the stars in the back of the truck after cookin' those Brookies over the campfire. We can do some 4-wheeling up there before we head back, too. What-da-ya think?"

"Wow. Those are amazing plans. I haven't been bowling in years. Sounds fun."

<hr>

In the midst of the smoky din, country music blasted, competing with the sounds of crashing bowling balls. "What did you say, Charlie?" Cricket yelled.

"How'd ya like the fish and chips?"

"Pretty tasty. Best I've had in a long while."

The couple they paired-up with—friends of Charlie's—teased Cricket about her bowling form. But she managed to finish the first game with a 145. Sadie, a short pudgy waitress with spiky bleached hair emptied the ashtrays and removed the empty beer bottles, then brought another round for the foursome.

"This round's from Rick." Sadie pointed to a tall cowboy with a pot belly. Rick nodded and tipped a black cowboy hat, decorated with a well-tooled hat band.

Charlie motioned for Rick as Cricket said, "Charlie, I hate to be ungrateful, but I really don't want any more beer. Please tell Sadie no more for me, no matter who orders one."

"Anything you say little lady. Hey, Rick, how ya doing? I'd like you to meet my gal, Cricket. She's here, clear from Colorado."

She wanted to refute the "my gal" part, but let it pass. How would she explain the oddity of their meeting because of a wrong phone number, and how she came to be "my gal" to a man she had not set eyes on until a few hours ago?

The rest of the evening was a noisy blur. Lots of jokes, laughter, and introductions. Cricket enjoyed watching the locals, who were friendly, but made side glances at this outsider. They knew how to have a good time and though she had a good time, this wasn't quite her domain. What was her domain?

Heading back toward Charlie's, the truck's gentle jostling amplified Cricket's weariness and she caught only snips and snatches of Charlie's banter. Her head jolted as the truck came to an abrupt stop. It took a few moments to unravel the tangle in her mind. Where was she?

Lowering the window, Charlie whispered, "Listen."

And she heard the chorus. The rhythmic trill of an ensemble of frogs. The see-sawing chirp of a few crickets. Both in harmony with the whistling breezes in a few nearby noble pines.

"What do you think? Crickets singing for Cricket. How 'bout that? Come on. It's a beautiful eve for a walk."

It *was* a glorious evening. And stretching her legs would chase away the drowsiness.

Rising from the peak silhouetted in front of them emerged the brilliance of the nearly full moon. Its illumination cast shadows of the couple as they meandered the downward trail. Aha, a pond. That was where the frog sounds came from. Easy ripples glistened, reflecting the moonlight. Cricket was awed by the view, the harmonious sounds and softness of cool air whispering across her face. As they reached the pond's edge, Charlies' massive hand caught Cricket's with its firm grip.

With Charlie and Cricket's intrusion, the night music halted. In a hushed voice Charlie spoke. "Miss Cricket, you sure make a man proud. Did you see how the folks couldn't keep their eyes off you tonight? Just being close to ya—and now out here in God's country—warms a man's heart."

Charlie released Cricket's hand and thrust his face and arms skyward. "Wow."

Cricket heard the grin in his voice and wondered how to respond. Yes, with the moon, the pond, and the critters, it was a wow scene.

His sudden move surprised her. With a tight embrace, he wrapped her and pulled her to him, burying her face in his chest. Trying to get a full breath, she turned her head to the side. His day's growth of whiskers caught in her hair.

Now, accustomed to the intruders, the frog and cricket choir resumed, louder Cricket thought, than before. She also heard the pa-pump, pa-pump of Charlie's heart. Cricket felt her heart pounding too. What was that all about?

Charlie's cheek brushed the loosened curls at her crown, and he swayed gently holding Cricket to him. Cricket's mind raced.

I don't want to disappoint him. He's tried so hard and has been so charming. It would be fun to do the fishing trip, camping and cooking out tomorrow. I've needed a nice outing for such a while. That's why I came. For a good outing. Right? But I don't want him having romantic ideas. Maybe I should take off after he's asleep and leave him a note. No, I couldn't do that to him.

His release was tender. Then he lifted her chin with two fingers, tipping her head toward him. In the moonlight she could see questioning in his shadowed eyes and crinkled brow.

"Charlie. I can't do this. I'm sorry."

"Did I do something wrong? Ya know, I'm not fixin' to have a roll in the hay. Promise. But I like being with you."

"You've been an angel, Charlie. And planned a wonderful time. Charlie bit on his lip and nodded.

⋄━━◆━━⋄

The spinning tires spit gravel in their wake as Charlie drove away from the night magic. Both remained silent. Maneuvering the curves and hills, Charlie hovered over the steering wheel, eyes fixed, jaw tight. Cricket wondered what was going through his mind. Her brimming eyes could no longer hold the salty tears. They tumbled onto prominent cheekbones and plopped into her lap.

Good grief, why was she feeling such tenderness? Or was she angry at herself for putting the two of them in this position?

Pulling up in front of his house, Charlie punched the light switch and extinguished the headlights. His place looked forlorn in the night shadows. He relaxed his fixed jaw and Cricket felt his warm hand pat her cool thigh moistened by her tears.

"Well Miss Cricket, let's hit the hay. We've got a big and exciting day ahead of us tomorrow." He wasn't giving up.

Inside, Charlie pointed to the pull-out couch. This here's where I'm sleeping. The sheets are clean and ready for you in the bedroom. You'll have it all to yourself."

He waved away her protests and eased a loose curl away from her sleepy eyes." Now you get your tail in that bedroom. A good sleep and you'll be fresh as a daisy."

Snuggled beneath the freshly laundered sheets she watched the digital clock flash from one-thirty and all the way to one-forty. What should she do? Sleep came reluctantly, but soundly.

Maybe it was the sliver of morning sun that crept along her cheek, or the whiff of brewing coffee that brought her to consciousness. Whatever it was, the fog of sleep cleared instantly.

A speedy shower and even speedier pat of foundation, puff of color for her cheeks, stroke of eye shadow, brush of smoky mascara, and she felt presentable. Cricket fastened her hair with a coral barrette that matched her peasant blouse covering all but a few inches of her beige shorts. When she padded barefooted into the sunlit kitchen, she thought it had lost some of its somberness.

"Well, lookie here. I bet you slept like a log. This morning you look like a peach blossom instead of a daisy. Coffee's ready. In fact, I'm on my second cup."

I've been smelling it since I woke up. I'd love some. And you're right, I did sleep like a log. Your bed was nice and comfy."

The coffee, strong as it was, tasted good as she sipped it from a giant mug. Charlie had his back to her fiddling with the microwave. His narrow body had its greatest width at his shoulders. He was dressed, as yesterday, in a long-sleeved cotton plaid western shirt buttoned snugly at the wrists. Jack had always worn long sleeves with two wide turn-backs that exposed his muscular forearms. She liked men's forearms. To her they displayed the strength and sexiness of a man.

Ding! Charlie removed a platter from the micro, displaying three of the largest cinnamon rolls, oozing with white juicy frosting, that Cricket had ever seen. Surely one would feed a family of four. "Goodness, Charlie. You expecting an army for breakfast?"

"These are Ma Jones' specialty. She has a little bakery down near the bowlin' alley and folks come fifty miles to get her rolls. I keep some in the freezer for special occasions." He nodded toward her. "Besides I didn't want to subject you to my old greasy bacon and eggs."

"This is perfect." She forked bite after bite of the sweet tender cinnamon morsel between sips of Charlie's brew.

There was small talk about the bowling and beautiful moonlight the night before and today's sunshine with a few billowing clouds forming in the north. Laying her fork down, Cricket leaned forward and caught Charlie's gaze with her own. "Charlie, I want to be honest with you."

Charlie licked his lips, closed them tight and cocked his head to one side, waiting for her to continue.

"I've been on automatic pilot ever since Jack's death. I've been a human doing and not much of a human being. I haven't let myself feel much." She looked down, gathering her thoughts. "This whole crazy thing of you accidently getting me on the phone, and now my being here with you has helped me begin to really feel again. I believe I'm turning a corner in my life. I thank you for being a part of that. I'm spreading my wings in a different way and reaching for new adventures."

"But not with me, huh?"

"Charlie, I'll always value and remember our phone friendship and my short time here with you. You are a very fine man."

"Friendship, huh?" She heard the hurt in his voice. "Well, I reckon I knew all along that you and me was too good to be true. Old rubes like me don't quite fit with the likes of you."

"Charlie…" She bit into her lower lip.

"Now Cricket, don't look so serious. Give me that lopsided grin. It's Ok. Your road just took a turn and I'm not part of it. That's life."

She flashed him her cockeyed smile, scooted the kitchen chair away from the table and stood. "I guess you're right Charlie."

"Now, don't run off too fast. I have something for you. Just wait right here." Charlie headed to his bedroom and returned in a few minutes with a bundle wrapped in a terrycloth towel. "It's something I've been working on for a while. When you decided to come, I hurried to finish it. I hope you like it."

Cricket reached out to grasp the awkward looking parcel. She carefully pulled away one corner of the towel and then another corner to reveal a well-carved bird, its wings—about 12 inches from tip to tip—positioned for flight. "I'm speechless. It's ... beautiful ... remarkable."

"It's a prairie falcon. And like you, it's fixing to take off. To soar."

◆

Her dusty silver bullet glided toward Colorado. Hey, she didn't have to rush. She braked to cut the cruise control and pulled to the side of the road. She reached to open the foil package and nibbled on the rest of Ma Jones' roll. Yum. Cricket eyed the carved prairie falcon perched beside her. She held it up and traced a finger over the layers of feathers on the outstretched wings. Yes, Charlie had helped to give her new wings.

FULL CIRCLE

Another disappointment. Andy stuffed his hands into his pockets and leaned into the icy wind stinging his cheeks and ears. He was so sure he would get the job, but Harvey's Wheels and Tires hired someone else with the usual explanation. "Sorry, you're overqualified." Layoffs had hit families hard and this was Andy's third month without a job. He worried about Angie and their soon-to-be-born baby. Her waitress job would not support them. The rent and utility bills had robbed all but $20 of their savings and the checking account hovered dangerously around $40.

At the intersection he waited for the walk signal. Two more places held slim promise. If neither paid off… He refused to think about it.

Careening around the corner, a car, sleek and black, passed in front of him. Something bulky, also black, rolled from the top of the car, over the trunk lid, and plunged into the street. Andy yelled out, but the car kept going. He leaped from the curb and managed to grab the woman's purse before another vehicle reached the crosswalk.

Andy's eyes searched in the direction of the retreating automobile and glimpsed the flash of brake lights as it turned the corner. Peering inside the bag, he saw a clutter of items, and nestled to the side was the fattest wallet he had ever seen. A flash of envy concerning the possible stash in the wallet washed over him. He shook his head and stifled his covetousness.

Maybe I can catch her. He bounded off down the block, skirting around and between pedestrians, both coming and going, all of whom gave him looks of irritation. At the intersection he paused, puffing steam in quick bursts. To the right he saw that she was already half a block ahead of him. *Got to catch the lady.* He raced between cars in the crosswalk and chased after the owner of the bag.

It took two blocks at full speed before Andy reached the shiny car. He heaved the bulky bag into the air again and again until the woman spotted him. She eased the auto next to the curb and lowered her window. Andy stared into a face crinkled in merriment. Disheveled fluffs of silver hair spilled from beneath a crocheted cap of purple and silver.

A giggle escaped the woman's throat before she spoke. "Golly jees young man. I believe you rescued my purse."

Andy's words exploded in bursts. "Saw it roll from … the top of your car… I'm glad… I could catch you."

"What a hero you are. Thank you. Thank you."

"It's nothing Mrs. …"

"Goldwin. Jan Goldwin."

"Here you are Mrs. Goldwin." Andy's breathing returned to normal as he nudged the oversized purse through the window toward its owner.

"I'm a little wacky. Can't believe I left my bag on top of the car. Just think what could have happened, losing all my identification, credit cards, money, and all." She fumbled with her wallet and opened it to a stack of bills. "You deserve a reward. Let me pay you."

"No. No. Please, Mrs. Goldwin. I don't want money. I'm just glad I was there at the right time."

"How can I thank you? Repay you for being so honorable?"

Andy studied his feet, then looked up and into the woman's eyes with his own, steady as Michelangelo's statue David. "I'd be honored … if you find a way to pass a good deed to a person in need. That's all."

Her protests became vanishing foggy breath in the icy cold. Andy stood firm.

"There's no changing your mind is there?" The fire in her eyes danced as she handed Andy a white box tied in vivid purple ribbon. "I'm delivering boxes of yummy toffee to shut-ins today. Please take this to remember your good deed. And… I will look for a person in need."

Despite the creeping puffiness of her ankles and the dragging fatigue, Angie continued to work the breakfast and lunch shift at the neighborhood Egg and I. She had to. Andy's lay off eliminated any choice in the matter. Little Bantam—would it be Annie or Anthony?—was due on Christmas Day. She wondered how they would remember this Christmas. Bleak? Or joyous?

Nearing the two o'clock closing time, as Angie straightened the condiments and menus on each table so they would be ready for the next day, the front door swooshed open. A customer loaded with multicolored packages rushed in.

She waved toward Angie and cried out, "Am I too late for lunch?"

An apron-clad man peaked out from the kitchen. Angie signaled with a thumbs-up. "I got this, Sam."

Angie hurried toward the women. "No, you have five minutes to spare. Here, let me help you with those packages. It looks like you've been doing a lot of shopping."

"That, and a long list of things. These are for my nieces and nephews. Didn't have time to take them to my car. I'll need to mail them soon."

Angie placed the packages on a nearby table. "Your nieces and nephews will love their presents. This one has something tinkly inside. For a boy, right? Dainty and pretty, this must be for a girl."

The woman grinned and settled in at the table. "Yup."

The last package stacked, Angie handed over the menu and then pressed the palm of her hand against the swell of her belly at the edge of her rib cage. *Hey, little guy, you've been pestering your mommy all day. Give me a break and get that foot outa my ribs.*

The patron fingered the menu before she spoke. "But look at you, soon to bring a new babe into the world. A boy or a girl?"

"We chose not to find out about our little Bantam ahead of time. I dream about holding a little bundle and watching blinking eyes and sleepy yawns. I just hope we can …" Her voice trailed off.

"You'll be a perfect mom." She chuckled and added, "I have good instincts."

"Thanks. You remind me of my great grandmother, the same twinkle in your voice. Of course, she's been gone a lot of years. She had a generous heart." Angie drew in a deep breath. "Well, we better get your order to kitchen. What will you have?"

<hr>

Eager as she was to get home and learn the news about the job at Harvey's Tires and Wheels, she hated to face the whirling cold. Her only winter coat was a failure at blocking out the bitterness, and she shivered at the memory of the morning walk. *It's only two blocks. Don't be such a weenie.* She had something incredible to share with Andy and this spurred her on.

Bracing for the expected blast, she gripped the door handle. Outside, a soft quietness surprised and surrounded her. Gone was the icy bite. Downy fluff made its lazy descent alighting on the barren branches, burying the brittle lawns, and muffling the sounds of the street. Snowflakes danced around her hurried stride, a stride of anticipation as she headed home.

The carport's empty. Darn. Angie turned the key in its lock and stepped inside. She wrinkled her nose at the familiarity of spicy aftershave. Andy had not been gone long. She removed her boots and shook the melting flakes from her coat, then draped it over a kitchen chair. On the table was a heavily scrawled message.

> **Angie honey,**
> **No go at Harvey's, but the last stop paid off.**
> **I start <u>tomorrow.</u>**
> **Home soon.**
> **We'll have Christmas after all.**
> **I love you and little Bantam.**
> **A**

Then she saw it. *Hmm. A box like mine.* Angie patted the place where a foot made a ripple across her belly. "Yeah, little Bantam, a job for Daddy. And joy all around us."

Angie gazed out the window to watch the gentle flakes find their place. *What would Andy say about the woman who ordered a chocolate* *shake and cream of asparagus soup, then left a box of toffee, all decorated pretty, a note, <u>and</u> four one-hundred-dollar bills?*

For the cheery waitress and little Bantam.
I'd be honored if you find a way to pass a good deed to a person in need.
Mrs. G.

THE FACE OF A SUNBEAM

By Carol Alford

I never know what to expect when I walk into an unknown classroom. Until I find a job as a permanent teacher, I bounce from one school to another as a substitute. Sometimes the students seem happy to have a new face in the classroom and I hear "Can you be our teacher everyday?... I can't believe how fast you learned our names...Boy I learned a lot today."

And other times no matter what I say or do the cry is something like "You should let us work together on assignments, *our* teacher does... Mr. X says we're not supposed to do all the problems, just the odd numbers... That's not the way we do it."

This October morning is gray as I await the students' arrival for first period. Class begins in five minutes, but experience tells me the students will not enter the room until the last second. I am proven wrong when a lone boy shuffles into the classroom. He tucks his chin and focuses his eyes on the floor. The denim cuffs of his pants swish the rhythm of his quick, short steps. He stops, stares at me with a frown. The face that initially seemed more like a bashful sunbeam has dissolved into a threatening cloudburst.

The swishing cuffs begin again and continue until they reach the front seat of the first row. The boy claims his desk and unzips his black binder to remove a slender children's book. I sense that he doesn't want me to see the side glances that he casts my way. Resolute, he focuses on turning one page, then another. His finger traces the printed words. *He's reading?* But pshu, pshu, pshu are the whispered sounds I hear.

He appears much younger than the ninth graders I expect to see today. Vulnerability oozes from him and I am touched by it. I clutch my chest to ease the heaving I feel inside.

How can I quiet the discomfort I sense from this child? Searching the seating chart, I find his name and approach his desk. I've been taught to get on the level of the child. I bend down and try to connect his eyes to mine. He is wary and flashes a darting glance. I am further stymied but give it a shot. I refuse to give up.

"Good morning, Danny. I'm Miss Tobin. I'm your substitute teacher today." I hope my voice is soothing and non-threatening and that my smile is welcoming.

His stubby fingers shove the book into the binder, and he slams it closed. The floor again becomes his focus. The whole of this young boy pulls at my heart. His wire-rimmed glasses, the tawny freckles sprinkled over his face, the carefully gelled corn-silk thatch, the ears that tend to flop, the quiver that lives on his lips.

Does it bother him that I'm leaning close to him? I move away and speak again. "Tell me about your book. Is it a good story? Do you like the pictures?"

Danny's eyes will not meet mine. He fingers the zipper tab of his binder. The quiver of his lip continues.

Ashamedly, I welcome the interruption when a boy, still growing into his feet, bursts into the room. "Hey, we have a sub. Hi Miss sub." The whole atmosphere explodes as chattering students find their seats. The girls in the back corner are the last to quiet down as I use the seating chart in checking attendance. Only one seat is empty.

I proceed with the lesson plan, yet my attempt to focus on the goals for the day is clouded by the boy I want somehow to reach. His slender book again lies open. The pshu, pshu pshu of this special student is the backdrop for each activity. There is a fifteen-minute video followed by a volley of questions. I toss a beanbag to a student and that student answers the first question then tosses the bag to another student.

'Throw it to me,' echoes from one side of the room to the other. I am surprised how eager each person is to get the bean bag and to give an answer. Danny is unaware of the blue and orange bag of beans, and no one throws it to him.

While the students write summary paragraphs during the last ten minutes of class, I orbit the room checking on their progress. The session goes fine, but I might as well have been a stick broom when it comes to reaching Danny. My eye once more lands on the lone green polo shirt hunched over the desk in the front corner of the room. Threatening tears and a sniffle gather with each of my breaths. It *could* be attributed to the cold that has been brewing in my sinuses.

Where are my tissues? I dig for one in my blazer pocket. It is beginning to disintegrate, but I use it anyway. Back turned, I'm hidden away from the students. The empty corner stares at me. My first blow honks in my ears and finishes one tissue in a gooey glob. Another pocket-dig produces a wad that catches the next two blows. They are not one whit quieter, but my head is clear, and the sniffs are gone.

The empty corner continues to be my refuge until I am startled to hear my three honks perfectly replicated. I turn to seek their origin. A grinning Danny with quaking shoulders looks me straight in the eye. Hunched over his desk he cups his thick pink hands around his nose and mouth, and twice more performs the impersonation.

"Are you teasing me?" I'm grinning too.

Danny giggles. He points to the story he is reading inviting me to move closer.

"See. The Punkin ghost."

He can talk. I'd wondered about that. "What's the punkin ghost doing?"

"Scarin the punkins." Danny's whole face is a sunbeam. "You here tomorrow?"

I wait for the tingles to reach the crown of my head. "Yes, Danny, I will be here tomorrow."

THE DAMSEL'S DESIRE

By Carol Alford

The apparition first visited me when I was four. Pretty in the face with old fashioned clothes, she stood squarely in front of the two-wheeler I peddled. I was the youngest on the block to ride. Mother said no one she knew gave up her training wheels as soon as I did. Everyone else, even my brother Harvey, didn't master the bicycle until he was seven. Anyway, saying that she stood isn't quite accurate since "The Damsel," as I later named her from some of my fairytale books, more like—*floated* above the graveled driveway. She made me mad, 'cause I nearly wrecked trying to avoid her, which was completely unnecessary. I could have ridden right through her in the first place.

Looking back, I still don't quite get why she chose that way to introduce herself. I mean, she could have waited till I was in bed for the night, after my bedtime story and when I was groggy with the twilight of sleep. Then she could have come like a dream. Don't you think that would have been less weird for a four-year-old?

I think I figured out why she started visiting when I was young. I mean I'm still young, just sixteen. But back then, make-believe was part of my life and I had all sorts of friends that snuggled with me or that I talked to—when I was by myself, mind you. There was Cornelius the unicorn, KoKo the gecko, Peedy the centipede and my only people-type, Con the leprechaun. No one else could see them or hear them except me. They were special. Cornelius with her glassy red eyes, pink horn, mane, and tail against a pearl white coat. KoKo, who changed from yellow to blue to green and always with sparkles. Well, you get the idea. So, when The Damsel showed up, I wasn't the least bit scared, just a little ticked about her invading my life. If she had first arrived when I was twelve when I'd given up my make-believe friends, I might have thought I was going bonkers or something.

She hasn't changed over the years—in looks that is. Still in the same dirndl dress of brown tones with red braid trim. When I learned about her heritage—from her of course—I looked up Austrian dress. Found it. Dirndl: a dress with a full gathered skirt and a tight low bodice that is worn over a short-sleeved blouse and is part of both German and Austrian national costume. Now that I'm a teenager, I'd say that she looks rather sensuous. Her brown hair is always flowing and a bit messy. Her eyes, vivid and a teasing blue. Though her mouth remains closed, almost in a pucker, I hear her voice—in my head, that is. It's low and liquid. I've tried to imitate it but can't.

So, what does she want with me? I'm not sure yet. It's not like she visits me regularly. I think she has a handle on my future however, you know, like she predicts what's coming. When I was in kindergarten, she sat on the teacher's desk blowing out candles that kept re-lighting. I thought it was kind of dumb. Then she said something puzzling. "Charlene Jenkins, no matter what happens, remember to take your jacket." That afternoon we had a fire and had to evacuate. Some sixth grader brought a lighter to school and lit the contents of a trash can. They said he was a troubled kid. We had to stand outside in the winter bitterness for a whole hour and I was the only one who had my jacket.

The Damsel visited me quite often the year I turned nine. It was a pretty rough year for our family. My thirteen-year-old brother was diagnosed with leukemia. She predicted Harvey's recovery. Actually, she instigated my role in that recovery. I remember him pale and thin, sprawled in the awkwardness of puberty across the hospital bed, trying to look brave. None of the treatments, mostly meds, were working.

The doctors recommended a bone marrow transplant. My parents, an aunt and two uncles volunteered to be tested, but they weren't a match. Harv, by now his preferred handle, usually full of witty comments, was silent one afternoon while I tried to make him laugh with stupid jokes. The Damsel appeared, rather comical really, dancing on the foot of the hospital bed. Some hippity-hop folk thing. She leaped onto the side chair and then to the window ventilation unit, swishing her skirt side to side to some imaginary rhythm. I almost burst out and told the whole thing to Harv and the nurse, who hovered over the IV she inserted into Harv's vein. How I wished Harv could feel her presence. I knew it'd lift his spirits. Then I heard it. "You'll be the donor."

My parents weren't too hip about my request to be tested. "You're too young to go through all that," they argued. But even at nine I wasn't one to be dissuaded. Harv and I shared similar protein molecules called Human Leukocyte Antigens to be a match. Even at nine I learned all the scientific terminology. Aren't you impressed?

Sure enough, just like The Damsel predicted, they sucked some hematopoietic stem cells from the bone marrow of my hip—not without some to-heck-and-back pain—and eventually we both recovered from the procedures. Harv was healed. The Damsel visited me a lot over those weeks, you can be sure, mostly just there with her sultry smile. I found it comforting.

You might imagine that I will forever be in the fine graces of Harv and my parents. They think it's a bigger deal than I do. The experience led me in a certain direction for a while. I wanted to be a doctor. As a junior, high school was good, and I continued as top kid in my class of 500 plus students. But I changed passageways. I loved science, but I didn't want to spend most of my life in a science classroom. I journeyed on a new path.

Again, The Damsel got me going in this fresh direction. I was grumping about my genetics test. I learn well, but this time I had to pull an all-nighter to prepare, since the school swim team had been taking so many hours away from my study. I might add that my goal is to place in the top three in the conference in two swim events this season, so training is imperative. Right? But I don't like doing all-nighters. Even a test score of 95% didn't ease my perturbance. Okay, that's not really a word, but I like to say it, anyway. So, I was griping and grimacing when The Damsel shimmied through the windshield of the car I call donkey, as she's a bit stubborn at starting. The Damsel says right out, "It's great for women to be scientists. But instead of being one, you should write about them."

And that's what I did. For the co-editor application, I needed to submit a story. In my research I found the name of Lise Mietner, an Austrian from Vienna, born in 1875. Hey, this is cool, I thought. That's where my apparition grew up. Remember she told me a long time ago. I surmise that she's from that era since her dress, the dirndl, remember? was particularly popular in Austria in the 1880s.

Although very few women were allowed to attend university back then, Lise's unrelenting go-get-um attitude got her accepted at Vienna University in 1901, and under the tutelage of her teacher, Ludwig Boltzmann—I love those foreign names—she discovered that physics was her calling. She was the first woman to graduate with a doctoral degree in physics from the University of Vienna. With doctorate in hand, she chose a famous institute in Berlin as her place of work. For 30 years she labored with Otto Hahn studying atoms, expanding the field of nuclear physics.

Sometimes men turn to women for answers, even back then. And that is what Hahn did. He wondered about the strange reaction he noted when observing uranium atoms. Lise discovered that tremendous energy could be released when atoms were split. Yet wouldn't you know it? Women's equality failed Lise Meitner. Even though she was the first to suggest nuclear fission, it was Dr. Hahn who received the Nobel Prize in Physics in recognition of the findings. Lise was ignored. However, later the element with atomic number 109 was named Meitnerium in her honor. I say, "Way to go, girl. Your discovery of nuclear fission has been used around the world, not only for weapons, but in the fields of energy and medicine."

As I wrote the essay about Lise Meitner, I pondered. Am I wise turning away from a medical or science field? Maybe I could be a modern-day Lise Meitner and discover how to transfer atoms and complete organisms over radio waves obliterating the need for gas to get us from place to place. Surely, they wouldn't deny me a Nobel Prize for something like that.

Well, back to The Damsel's continuing premonitions. After I wrote the Lise Meitner essay, she came to me in the night. I'm still circling the fort about it, not getting the gist of it. It wasn't what she told me, but the way she came. Many times, I couldn't see her whole body, maybe only to her waist and sometimes to the hem of her dirndl. Usually, she came in a haze and appeared rather filmy, but this time all I saw was her blurry head and tousled hair, even more unruly than usual. Her message was quick but clear—you'll be the co-editor—and she was gone.

Maybe she had others to visit. That never occurred to me. I assumed I was her only contact in the real flesh. Regardless, as she declared, the journalism teacher/newspaper sponsor liked my essay, and wal-la, I became co-editor. We instituted a contest for essays about women scientists and their contributions. We have students trying to find the most interesting story, and so far, we've run four of them. Don't worry, the co-editor and I are not feminists. The contest showcasing male scientists starts next month.

Well, the years have passed and it's time to resume my story. Throughout high school I was known as Charly. It seemed to fit my bounce around life. Some old friends continue with the moniker, however presently as a writer in my late twenties, Charlene A. Jenkins, and the A doesn't stand for Ann, seems more professional.

Wouldn't you know? I write scientific articles for professional periodicals. I'm forever interviewing researchers and naturally doing mega piles of reading on the subjects I cover, such as glucose metabolism and early onset Alzheimer's, or cybernetic implants in the brain to aid those who are paralyzed. I just finished a series relating to how depression and anxiety affect hormones, body chemistry, and ultimately relate to illness and other health problems. Hey, I need to be prepared for anything I might face. Right? And I need to make a living, you know.

Now let me catch you up concerning the years after becoming co-editor of the high school paper.

The encounters with The Damsel grew less and less. I stewed over it for a while, thinking I must have disappointed her in some way. On the other hand, I was grateful for more privacy. I never knew when she might appear, and I often felt like someone was looking over my shoulder. The last vision I had was after the junior prom. Can you believe I was nominated for prom queen? I hadn't thought of myself as queen material, but I didn't know how to refuse the nomination.

Boys were great as friends, but at that time studying and swimming swallowed most of my time. I did earn a first in freestyle and a second in the fly that year. So, there was no boyfriend to attend prom with. Susanna and I decided to go without dates. Going stag wasn't a completely unknown thing to do. I could tell that my parents were silently horrified, but they didn't say so.

Two weeks before the event, I had just pulled a frozen pizza—the only kind I knew how to make—from the oven. With music playing full blast, I gyrated to the frenzy beat, never missing a bite as I chomped away. In my adolescent fantasy I was a slinky dancer and I had shed everything except my bra and low-slung panties. I felt the glare of The Damsel before I saw her. She had parked herself cross-legged on the refrigerator and looked down her nose at me. In defiance I made a move that my father would definitely call suggestive, refusing to feel embarrassed by my unabashed behavior. After all, this was the privacy of my own home. I was alone for the night, and I could be anything I wanted. I grabbed another slab of pizza and continued my exhibition of sensuality into the family room. Thinking back, I'm sure the pizza-eating detracted from the appeal of my dance. This time she hovered beneath the vaulted ceiling and laughed and laughed, her mouth fully open.

I don't know how long I would have gone on in my liberating fervor, nor can I imagine how long she would have continued laughing, but I was interrupted by the doorbell. It was a set up alright, and I'm positive she knew about it. I scurried like a bunny whose scent had been discovered as the hound's snout nosed its hiding place under a rotting log when I snagged my hoodie and jeans heaped on the floor. The ringer of the doorbell was impatient. Hopping on one foot, trying to stab the other into the right leg took several tries, and in the end, the hoodie wound up inside out.

I stared through the locked screen door at the persistent doorbell ringer. A blast of porch light, the brilliance of a train's headlight, hit him full force. His stance, a swagger of you-finally-made-it, paired with dancing eyes of mischief, were only the tip of the iceberg when it came to appeal. Dimples, a ruffled, russet-colored head of hair, an impressive depth of chest *and* the dozen yellow roses he brandished, added chunks to the total hunk.

"I was afraid I got the wrong house. It's been a while, hasn't it? Brandon Phillips. My Mom's Linda," he said.

Of course, I knew Linda, my mom's best friend. Her son Brandon had attended the high school across town, was two years my senior and was on scholarship at the university. We used to hang out when our parents attended the same activity, a wedding, an athletic event, or a summer outdoor concert. Standing in the floodlight on my doorstep, he looked, well, like maybe guys could be a part of my life after all.

I gave him my toothiest smile hoping that he wouldn't focus on my greasy hair that needed a shampoo, and the inside-out hoodie. Oh well, teenagers are often into grunge, I thought. I stuttered a little when I said, "Brandon, my parents should be back soon. Do you want iced tea, a soda or something?" I couldn't say beer because we didn't usually have it in the house.

"I can't stay long. But I didn't come to see them. I came to see you."

Inside, I plopped the roses in a vase and filled it with water, which was the best I could do at arranging the fragrant blooms. Brandon's composure impressed me. He made his mission to ask me to the junior prom seem as natural as it would have been if we had been dating for years, and it was just a matter of nailing down the arrangements. I didn't consider turning him down, but I wondered what Linda promised Brandon if he did this favor for her best friend. After all, no mother wanted her daughter to be part of prom royalty without a date. Mom's motherly concern would be assuaged.

Subsequent to an appropriate time of catching up on each other's lives, and nailing the details of the evening, dinner at 7:00 at *Johnny*

Carinos—I was glad he didn't suggest *The Caverns* or some other equally elite and expensive spot—the dance at 8:30 and the after-prom party at 1:30. I properly gushed over the beautiful roses, the first of several I have received since, and we said our appropriate goodbyes.

Perhaps if I ever have a daughter, I will understand the exhilaration my mother expressed during our shopping venture and the over-the-top funds she was willing to rob from her budget for the dress. We chose cerulean blue satin which went with my eyes and rosy beige skin. The lines were simple and sleek, but not at all sexy, which I was bent on avoiding.

Not particularly a romantic, I spent little time imagining the wonder of the approaching evening. However, when Brandon arrived in his black tux and cerulean cummerbund—I'm sure our mothers collaborated on that—offering the typical well-coordinated corsage, it did catch my breath a little. And when he revved up the sporty, silver something we were riding in, I imagined that Cinderella and I shared some of the same sensations.

Brandon claimed he hadn't taken any dance lessons, but wow did he know the steps. Most of my friends stood in a spot that might have been marked by an X and never moved off of it, grinding and gyrating to the throbbing beat. But we—somehow in his arms I found the right way to move my feet in harmony with his—twirled, scooped, and swooped dozens of times around the floor. I never knew dancing could be so fun, and so good at getting the blood pumping, even though my body steamed like an aerobics instructor at the end of a session.

After the crowning, we had a slow dance, me with my tiara. Yes, I was the one who got crowned. Two more slow dances followed. I felt, well, queenly and a little special. The hormones did their damage and my whole being filled with tingles, especially when Brandon's lips brushed my neck, cheek and finally my lips. Just before the closing hour we left to get some fresh air. That was a mistake. Starry, with the glow of a full moon, the night skies spawned a well of passion.

By the time we crawled into the cramped back seat of the car, steamy kisses and wandering caresses had taken over. I'd kissed and made out a little before, but it hadn't moved me much. Brandon's "Oh, you're beautiful, you feel so good," turned into light moans, not unlike the ones I emanated.

Pushing away, I drew in a fresh breath, or as fresh as it could be in the fogged-up car. He grinned and touched his finger to the tip of my nose. I pulled forward from my crushed-against-the-corner position and saw *her* face jutting through the side window. Damn. The Damsel left no message. She merely gazed, a pensive one, until the vision grew shadowy, and only a wisp of mist lingered. Then she was gone and that was the last time I saw her for a long while.

About Brandon. We're both practical people and after prom we pursued our goals yet kept a long-distance relationship. He finished pre-med, med school and is now completing a residency in Maryland. I graduated high school with an A average, but didn't make valedictorian, since I took fewer advanced placement classes than some of the other students. It was my choice and I think I ended up with a more rounded course of study. Our school newspaper garnered several national awards my senior year and the notoriety led to a scholarship in journalism which covered tuition and books.

Each year the first weekend in May I receive a dozen yellow roses in remembrance of our first date. When Brandon and I see each other, it's fireworks all over again. Our moms are pushing us to set a wedding date. Maybe in the fall.

Brandon's the only one who knows about The Damsel. He's not sure he understands the whole thing and maybe I don't either, but when I tell him the latest…well, I believe he can accept it.

You see, though the apparition is no longer there, her voice has come back. She has been telling me her life story. I now know her desire. *She wants me to be her voice, to tell her story.* I have no idea why I don't see her anymore. Maybe she came as a vision in the beginning to get my attention, thinking I would have ignored her if she were only a voice. I do have a sketchpad from high school, the one with numerous pencil drawings of The Damsel, not that I need to look at them. I will never forget her face, her traditional dress, and her vitality. I believe they will help me visualize her as I write.

The Damsel has begun her storytelling, and I am in the process of determining how to put it on the page. She calls herself Gerda. Born to a peasant family, her parents knew right off that she was brilliant. She mastered the violin at a young age, learned languages easily and read everything she could find. Gerda's mother worked as a maid for Wilhelm Freiberg, a prominent high school teacher who taught at Leopoldstädter Kommunal-Realgymansium. Had to look that up for the spelling. This good fortune allowed Gerda to read and study many books borrowed from the teacher's library.

Gerda often accompanied her mother to the Freiberg's home and spent hours in the kitchen pouring over many of Freiberg's scientific papers. Wilhelm Freiberg took an interest in the young intellect and when Gerda was eleven, she and Freiberg began a discourse concerning neurology, which Gerda found fascinating. Freiberg went to bat for her and eventually arranged for her—posing as a boy—to take the entrance exam for the prominent gymnasium. Therefore, at twelve she began her studies alongside other fine students. In her final two years at the school, she shucked her boy's clothing and was recognized as the bright female Gerda.

Her words came to me, and I keyed them onto my computer. *I might have been the great collaborator. I do believe I might have left a mark in history. It all started in a fortuitous manner because of my contact with Wilhelm Freiberg. The fact that my beginnings were meager made no difference. I had come to believe that my life was charmed. You might also believe so when you learn that the first student I met at the gymnasium shared my birthdate, May 6, 1856. Sigmund Freud had been attending since he was nine and I entered at twelve. We became study partners. He didn't mind that when we first met, I masqueraded as a boy which made my acceptance at the gymnasium a reality. In fact, he found it amusing. We shared an interest in neurology and for years shared a comradeship unusual for such youngsters and later young adults. We even studied together for our Matura.*

Gerda told me that at seventeen, she graduated the Matura with honors and began her studies at Vienna University. Recording bits about her life made me smile. The research I had done concerning Lise Meitner in high school came back to me. Gerda also studied in Vienna, but nearly twenty years earlier. Interesting. The rigid schedule of studies, the intense desire for learning, and the study partnership she forged with fellow student Sigmund Freud at the gymnasium energized her.

When Gerda's voice faded, I put her story away and finished my latest submission, an article concerning immune-based drug treatment for cancer. It was past midnight when Gerda's voice came into the room once again, at first slow and liquid as I was accustomed, then in the rush and sound of a fierce windstorm. My readiness for a good sleep flew out the window. I frantically turned on my computer. My fingers danced in my efforts to keep up with Gerda's words.

Sigmund and I left the physiology lab after dark, and I refused his offer to escort me to my flat. Independence has always been a beneficial virtue of mine. Not so, this time. Surely if I had accepted his offer, this treachery would not have fallen over me. I remember turning the corner to my flat. The last stone's throw of distance—a space of darkness— never alarmed me. I detected movement near a dark stairway and hurried my pace. Someone grabbed me from behind, threw me to the cobblestones and pressed a chloroform-soaked cloth over my mouth and nose.

I remember nothing after the attack. Until now. I'm in the dim of a cellar. Cords fastened to ceiling beams coil around my wrists, holding me fast. My body dangles as my toes barely touch the floor. Tingling numbness overcomes my palms and fingers. The snug bodice of my dress tightens in this hanging position, and I find breathing difficult. Perhaps that is a blessing and protects me from the stifling putrid molecules hovering around me. Rats dig among the rags—stained black with dried blood—on the dirt floor in front of me. They venture close, their wild eyes taunting me. One nips at my ankle. I jerk and it retreats.

Two wooden slabs attached to heavy chains suspend from their own ceiling beams, and form floating tables. One holds a female corpse, skinned, sliced, and opened to expose any number of muscles, bones, and organs. I smell rotting flesh, though I can tell she has been doused with formalin in an attempt to slow the decomposition. One table is empty. I have never before tasted fear.

My abductor speaks from a dark corner. "Ah, you awaken. You can be proud to provide such an important role in understanding neurology my pretty one. You will be my youngest patient."

Oh, no! Charles. We had been forced to share a cubicle in laboratory for our physiology class. I have never liked him and had refused his attempts at conversation. He is overly crude and untidy. He imagines himself as the world's greatest gift to women and the world's greatest future scientist, when loathsome is what he is.

"Don't be afraid pretty one. You won't feel a thing. I need to leave for a short time. But I will return with my sketching materials."

The Damsel's voice trails away. My fingers freeze and then slip from the computer keyboard. The stinging of a thousand nettles burns my eyes. A suffocating chemical invasion assaults my throat. I fall to the floor in anguish, experiencing Gerda's deadly plight.

I yell to the ceiling. "Speak to me Gerda and I will write, I promise."

I throw myself across my bed. My head fills with questions. Did she escape? Did the abductor Charles mutilate her body under the guise of science? Will I ever know? Will I fulfill The Damsel's desire? Surely if Gerda wants me to write her story, she will reveal the ending.

Sleep finally comes to me, but fitfully. At early morning, sunrise sneaks into the room, a rosy glow. Peace overcomes me as I open my eyes. I move to my writing table and turn on my computer. A filmy vision perches on my dresser. Shocked to see her once again I blink and toss my head. Yes, it is Gerda, knees pulled up under her chin, smiling with the pucker I remember so vividly.

Oh, yes. I outsmart the vile Charles. When he returns and cuts me down, I fall as a limp sack of flour to the floor, unmoving. In the study of neurology, I learned how to slow my heart rate. I stare unflinching into his face as he kneels over me. "Oh, pretty one, don't leave me so soon. Perhaps this is for the best."

Charles drags me toward the empty floating table. He is stronger than I imagined and lifts me as if cradling a baby and places me with care on the table. It sways. I want to close my eyes to ward off dizziness. I wait. He turns away to set up an easel and position his drawing board. He hums an eerie tune. The feeling has returned to my hands and my movement is swift and silent. I pull the icepick from its hiding place, a decorative leather sash at my waist.

He returns to the table. "Now, pretty one, time to undress your lovely body."

I blink. He straightens up in surprise, only a moment before the pick penetrates deep into his heart. I've never displayed such force of strength. He falls back to the floor and grabs at his chest. His body shudders, then moves no more.

My fingers pause on my keyboard. Gerda, why did you come to me? What am I to tell? She sits cross-legged on my bed and smiles.

I finished my life. And you must finish yours. I returned to the home of my birth. A renewed joy and happiness came to me. I married Steffon, a strong and dedicated farmer. We raised four beautiful children. We left them the legacy of love, learning, and spreading goodness to the next generations. I could have remained cooped up in a lab doing experiments my whole life, but for me a greater fullness abounded. You and your Brandon will do the same as you raise your two sons and one daughter.

Hours later, I placed the last period on Gerda's story. Then I called Brandon.

"Will you marry me soon? We're going to raise two sons and a daughter."